Jimmy got up and put his arms around her. "Hey, I'm sorry."

She looked up at him, trembling, loving the way his arms around her made her feel so secure. So safe.

He touched her face. "I'm sorry I wasn't there, Candice."

She nodded. "Me, too."

Before she knew what had come over her, she stood on her tiptoes and kissed him. And it felt so right to kiss him again. Warmth spread through her and she melted in his arms all over again. The kiss deepened.

You need to end this.

Only, she couldn't. She didn't want to.

Dear Reader,

Thank you for picking up a copy of *A Reunion, a Wedding, a Family*.

I love to revisit places I have been, and revisiting Jasper was like a trip down memory lane.

Candice did have some big dreams, but when her family needs her, she stays and takes care of them. She gives up her dreams of becoming a doctor, loses her first husband and loses everyone she ever loved, but her life on the mountain makes it worthwhile. She saves lives and runs a tight ship at Mountain Rescue. That is, until a certain ghost from her past comes walking through her door.

Jimmy had left Jasper and joined the armed forces. He never planned on coming back to his hometown, but now he's a single dad and he has to do right by his son. He goes home and finds out the girl he's always loved, the girl he left behind, is now his boss. Now might be the chance to make his dreams come true, but he doesn't want to hold her back.

Neither of them forgot each other, and even after ten years, their love still burns.

I hope you enjoy Candice and Jimmy's story.

Amy

A REUNION,
A WEDDING, A FAMILY

———

AMY RUTTAN

HARLEQUIN

**MEDICAL
ROMANCE**

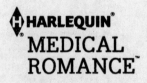

HARLEQUIN®
MEDICAL
ROMANCE™

Recycling programs
for this product may
not exist in your area.

ISBN-13: 978-1-335-14977-0

A Reunion, a Wedding, a Family

Copyright © 2020 by Amy Ruttan

This edition published by arrangement with Harlequin Books S.A.

For questions and comments about the quality of this book, please contact us at CustomerService@Harlequin.com.

Harlequin Enterprises ULC
22 Adelaide St. West, 40th Floor
Toronto, Ontario M5H 4E3, Canada
www.Harlequin.com

Printed in U.S.A.

Born and raised just outside Toronto, Ontario, **Amy Ruttan** fled the big city to settle down with the country boy of her dreams. After the birth of her second child, Amy was lucky enough to realize her lifelong dream of becoming a romance author. When she's not furiously typing away at her computer, she's mom to three wonderful children, who use her as a personal taxi and chef.

Books by Amy Ruttan

Harlequin Medical Romance

First Response

Pregnant with the Paramedic's Baby

Cinderellas to Royal Brides

Royal Doc's Secret Heir

Hot Greek Docs

A Date with Dr. Moustakas

The Surgeon King's Secret Baby
A Mommy for His Daughter
NY Doc Under the Northern Lights
Carrying the Surgeon's Baby
The Surgeon's Convenient Husband
Baby Bombshell for the Doctor Prince
Reunited with Her Hot-Shot Surgeon

Visit the Author Profile page
at Harlequin.com for more titles.

For all the positive strong women in my life.
This one is for you.

PROLOGUE

Summer, ten years ago
Jasper, Alberta

CANDICE WARNER HAD to put some distance between herself and her brother's antics. She loved Logan, but he was currently running around a campfire buck naked in the moonlight and she didn't need to see that. Especially not on her birthday.

Not that she couldn't understand or empathize with his desire to let loose tonight. In a week he and his best friend, Jimmy, would be leaving Jasper for basic training with the Canadian Armed Forces.

Jimmy. The boy she'd had a crush on forever.

Candice sighed. She was still processing the fact that Logan and Jimmy were leaving and she had no idea when she'd see them again.

You're leaving soon, too. You're going to university.

Even that was hard to process. It scared her. The idea of leaving Jasper was overwhelming. She'd spent her whole life here.

She wandered away from the campsite and sat down on a log by the river, far enough away to get some peace and quiet, so she could think. The only problem was, she couldn't think clearly. Her mind was going a mile a minute—everything was so uncertain.

"What're you doing here all alone?"

Candice glanced up to see Jimmy walking toward her. Her heart skipped a beat at the sight of him, like it always did. He had the reputation of being the love-'em-and-leave-'em type—always a new girl on his arm—which should have stopped her, but she couldn't help herself. There had always been something there—a spark, a connection—and she could talk to him in a way she couldn't with anyone else. She saw Jimmy for who he really was and she considered him one of her best friends.

For so long it had always been the three of them: her, Logan and Jimmy.

Now, with everyone leaving, nothing would ever be the same.

"Can I join you?" he asked, interrupting her

thoughts and making her realize she hadn't answered his initial question.

"Sure."

"Want a beer?" he asked, handing her a can.

She cocked an eyebrow. "I just turned nineteen an hour ago."

"Right, so you're legal now. And I thought you might need it after seeing your brother naked."

She laughed and took the can, but didn't open it. "Thanks."

Jimmy took a seat next to her and glanced up at the sky. "Wow. So many stars. I'm going to miss this."

"I'll bet." Candice sighed, hoping her voice wasn't shaking. She wanted to tell Jimmy how she felt, but couldn't find the words. And that was the problem—she had never been able to find the words. "So you and Logan are really leaving?"

Jimmy nodded. "There's nothing to keep us here."

"What do you mean there's nothing keeping you here?" she asked.

"Exactly that? What's the alternative? Work in my parents' motel and have no life, killing myself for ungrateful tourists? No thanks."

"Your parents worked hard to build the motel into a success."

He snorted. "Right. Which is why I was left alone most of my life."

"There's really nothing that makes you want to stay here?" she asked.

He chuckled. "Come on, Candy. What's here?"

"I am," she whispered, her body trembling as she found the courage to look him straight in the eye. "I'm here."

He smiled at her, his eyes twinkling in the moonlight. "Not for long. You're going off to school to become a doctor, some hotshot surgeon. You won't come back after that. You're too special to waste your life here."

Her cheeks heated. "What do you mean?"

Jimmy reached out and touched her face. She closed her eyes, her body humming with anticipation.

"I think you know what I mean, Candy," he said softly. And then he leaned in and pressed his lips against hers, stealing her first kiss.

She always wanted it to be him. Only ever him.

And in that moment, she didn't care that her brother had told her time and time again that Jimmy was off-limits.

This is what she had always wanted and she

wasn't going to miss her chance. She didn't want him to leave without knowing how she felt.

"I love you, Jimmy," she murmured against his lips.

"I love you, too, Candy. I always have."

Her knees went weak at his admission and she felt like she was going to cry. They kissed again. More fervently this time. They were both leaving but they had this last week together and she was going to make it count.

"Come on," she said, standing and reaching out a hand to him.

"Where are we going?" he asked.

"To my tent."

"Are you sure?" he asked. "Maybe it's the beer talking…"

"I haven't had a drop. Have you?"

"No." He showed her his can, which was unopened, just like hers. "I haven't had mine, either. I haven't had a drop all night."

"Then why did you bring me one?" she asked.

"To give me an excuse to come talk to you." He stood and cupped her face, kissing her again. "Because I couldn't leave without telling you how I feel."

"Come on," she said again, pulling on his hand and leading him to her tent.

"Are you sure, Candy?"

She nodded. "Yes."

She'd never been so sure of anything in her life.

CHAPTER ONE

Present day
Jasper, Alberta

"SO GLAD YOU'RE BACK, Candice!" Samantha greeted her warmly, as she approached the reception desk at Mountain Rescue.

"I'm glad to be back," Candice replied. And she was. After having a flu that had knocked her sideways for two weeks it felt good to be back at work, especially as she knew there was going to be so much to catch up on.

"You'll be happy to hear that the head office in Gatineau hired you a new paramedic while you were off sick. He starts today and should be here soon!"

Candice nodded as the receptionist handed her a file folder on her new employee.

"I told them I would get around to it," she muttered as she took a sip of her now cold coffee. Since she'd arrived an hour ago, she'd been busy trying to get through the thing she hated most: bureaucratic paperwork.

She would much rather be out in nature or in the field saving lives, but since she'd been promoted, she'd found herself stuck behind a desk more often than not. They were approaching the busy tourist season, though, so she was hoping that she could get out more. Just like she had in the winter, when all the skiers had descended upon Jasper and she'd had the chance to fly her helicopter a few times for rescues.

"I know, but they were approached by someone who's served in the Canadian military and had amazing credentials. They couldn't turn him down," Samantha said sympathetically. "I know you would've rather chosen your new paramedic yourself."

Candice's frustration ebbed away. She had a soft spot for anyone who'd served, like Logan had. Though she missed her brother terribly, she knew he would have been honored to have died in service to his country and she was so proud of everything he had accomplished. Her parents had been proud, too, before they passed—her mother a year after Logan was killed in action five years ago, her dad last summer, to pancreatic cancer.

So, yeah, she had a soft spot for those in the

military. Just thinking about Logan made a lump form in her throat. It was all she could do to stop herself from shedding a tear right there, but she made a point of not crying at work.

In fact, she never, ever cried in front of anyone.

Her ex-husband, Chad, had always said crying was a form of weakness. She was the boss here at Mountain Rescue. She couldn't afford to show weakness.

"Ex-military?" she asked, clearing her throat and trying to regain control of her emotions.

"Honorably discharged." Samantha smiled. "It can't be all that bad, can it?"

Candice nodded and half smiled. "No, you're right."

Head office knew what they were doing, even though she did prefer to make her own decisions about personnel.

Candice opened the file and was grateful she'd put down her coffee cup first. If she had been holding it, she would've dropped it right there, all over her paperwork.

Blaring up at her in big, bold letters was a ghost from her past.

"You okay?" Samantha asked.

Candice shook her head and quickly shut the file. "What?"

Samantha cocked an eyebrow. "I asked if

you were okay. It looked like you'd seen a ghost."

She tried to muster a smile, but it probably looked a little manic since Samantha took a step back from her.

"I'm fine. Could you let me know when he gets here?" She hoped that her voice wasn't shaking.

"Of course." Candice turned from the reception desk to head into her office, and only when the door was closed behind her did she relax, sitting down and opening the file again to stare at the name.

Jimmy Liu.

Samantha had been right about one thing— a ghost from her past *had* been contained in that new personnel file.

Jimmy was back.

Her first.

First kiss.

First time.

First love.

And her first broken heart. They'd spent a week together, just the two of them, and right before he left, he broke it off, shattering her heart. The memory of that moment came back to her in a painful flash.

"I thought you loved me?" she'd said that

day, a decade ago. Her heart had felt as if it was being crushed. It had been hard to breathe.

"I don't." He glanced away, not even having the decency to look her in the eye.

"So that's it?" she asked, her voice trembling.

"Yeah," he'd said, coolly. *"It is."*

Her heart had been shattered a second time months later when she'd lost the baby they had conceived that first night together.

Jimmy had never come back to Jasper again.

It had crushed her. Logan had warned her so many times about Jimmy, but she hadn't listened.

"Candy, Jimmy is my best friend, but he's not right for you," Logan had argued, trying to hold her back from going to see him that last night, after he'd broken things off.

"Let me go," she argued back. *"He loves me. He said he did."*

Logan looked at her sadly and her heart sank.

"Please, Logan. I need to talk to him."

He sighed. *"Fine, but honestly, Candy, you're too good for Jimmy. You have all these high aspirations and I think you need to pursue your dreams. You want to be a doctor. People like me and Jimmy...we'd just hold someone like you back,"* he'd concluded.

Now, Candice shook away that thought, tears stinging her eyes as she thought of Logan. As she thought of the rejection, the heartbreak and the dreams she hadn't followed.

Of the baby she lost.

The family she no longer had.

After losing Logan and her mother in the space of a year, it fell to Candice to stay in Jasper and take care of her dad. Even though he told her to go back to medical school, she couldn't leave him.

So Mountain Rescue had become her family. All she needed. They'd been the ones there for her when her father passed away last year.

Unlike her ex-husband.

And Jimmy.

Jimmy Liu. Back after all this time.

With a sigh, she set down the file and stood up, stretching and tying back her long, dark brown hair. She wandered over to the window that overlooked the parking lot and watched as an old, beat-up white SUV slowly parked.

An SUV she recognized from ten years ago.

Her pulse began to race, and when the door of the vehicle opened, her heart skipped a beat, just like it always did when she saw Jimmy.

You're the boss. Remember that. You're the one in control this time.

And she would keep reminding herself of

that. After Jimmy's rejection and her brief, disastrous marriage to Chad, she was done being rejected and hurt.

Everyone left her eventually, so she would never put her trust in someone else again. She'd never put her heart in someone else's hands.

Jimmy and Chad had both hardened her heart to love. So now her love was her work.

She took a deep breath to calm her frayed nerves. This was not how she wanted to start her Monday.

"The new paramedic is here," Samantha said, opening the office door.

"Thanks, Samantha. Show him in." She tried to keep her tone level.

Samantha nodded and disappeared.

Candice took another deep calming breath and took a seat behind her desk, straightening the papers and folding her hands across his file, her back ramrod-straight and her lips pursed tightly together. Nothing from the waist up betrayed the fact that her leg was twitching under the desk, nervously bouncing, while her pulse thundered between her ears.

Samantha returned, with Jimmy. "Right this way, Mr. Liu."

"You can just call me Jimmy," he said in that suave, charming voice that had won her over. The sound conjured up the image of his smile, the little twinkle in his dark eyes and the inevitable wink.

She'd fallen for that charm once.

But that was then and this was now.

You've got this. You're the boss, remember? You hold the power this time.

She rolled her shoulders as he walked into the room, but the moment he appeared, all that resolve, all the control she had over herself, seemed to melt away, like the morning mist off the lakes when the summer sun hit it.

He looked almost exactly the same, but he had filled out in all the right places. Broad-shouldered and muscular, the grey suit and white dress shirt he wore fit him like a glove. His black hair was short and clean-cut and there was a small scar on his face, but that handsome chiseled jaw and those full lips were just the same as she remembered.

Lips she had often dreamed about in the years after he left. She could still remember their first kiss down by the river so clearly. The night he'd taken her in his arms and she put her heart in his hands, giving herself to him.

Trusting him not to hurt her.

Listening to him whisper that he'd always love her.

Lies.

Don't think like that.

He flashed one last smile at Samantha and then his gaze fell on Candice, his eyes widening and his mouth opening in shock for a brief moment.

She was very thankful that he couldn't see her leg tapping under the desk. He'd know she was nervous then. She put a hand on her knee to stop herself.

"Candy?"

"Jimmy Liu," she said. "It's been a long time."

Jimmy couldn't quite believe what he was seeing and for one brief moment he was reminded of all those old black-and-white movies that his yéye would watch endlessly when he was kid.

"Of all the gin joints in all the world, she had to be in mine..." Or something like that.

Right now, he was feeling that.

Hard.

Gone was that shy, shrinking girl he'd once known. The one always hiding behind Logan or behind a book. Here sat a confident woman. Her hair was still that beautiful, silky brown and the sight of it reminded him of the few times he'd tucked a strand behind her ear, making her blush.

He couldn't help but wonder if she still bit

her bottom lip when she was nervous, something he had always found endearing.

Seeing her brought him right back to that
night when they'd first kissed, the night they'd
made love.

God, he'd loved her then.

He would've stayed with her. If it hadn't
been for Logan.

"You can't see my sister," Logan had snapped,
pushing him.

"What do you mean?" Jimmy asked. *"I love
her. It's why I can't enlist with you. I want to
stay with her."*

Logan shook his head. *"She has dreams,
dude. Dreams to become a doctor. You'd hold
her back."*

Jimmy sighed. He knew Candice had big
plans—it was one of the things he admired
most about her. *"But I love her."*

"If you love her, Jimmy, you'll let her go,"
Logan had said. *"Let her go. For me."*

He shook the memory from his mind and
saw the way her dark brown eyes were looking at him confidently, not darting around nervously.

Logan had made it clear that Candice was
off-limits, and even though Jimmy knew it was
for the best, it had killed him to walk away
from her. He'd carried a picture of her—stolen

from Logan—with him for years. He still had it. Thinking of her and her better life without him had gotten him through the heartache and loss.

Especially when he'd learned she'd married.

Jimmy may have failed Logan on the front lines—he'd survived that IED attack, but hadn't been able to save his best friend's life—but he could keep that old promise he'd made before they left Jasper ten years go. He'd let Candice go so she could follow her dreams and she was still off-limits. Even if a part of him still wanted her, was still affected by her.

She's married.

Not that he was even in a position to think about dating or being with anyone. He'd sowed his wild oats and he was paying for it now. He had responsibilities and a son who depended on him.

"It's Candice, not Candy," she said, sternly interrupting his thoughts. "And when we're out in the field we address each other by our surnames, so you can call me Lavoie."

His stomach knotted. Lavoie—so that was her married name. He was somehow envious of her husband, while also hating the man's guts.

"That's why I didn't recognize your name,"

Jimmy said. "Lavoie and not Warner. How long have you been married?"

He knew, of course. She had gotten married just a month before the IED attack in the Middle East. It was a peacekeeping mission that had gone sideways, injuring him and killing Logan.

Jimmy had spent months recovering in a military hospital in Germany, undergoing surgery to remove shrapnel from his hip and learning to walk again as both his legs had been broken.

And the whole time, all he could think about was how his best friend was dead and the girl of his dreams was someone else's wife.

Her eyes narrowed as a blush rose in her cheeks. "I'm divorced, but didn't bother changing my name back."

"Oh." Secretly he was thrilled, but he tried not to show it.

He recalled her words to him... *I love you, Jimmy. I always have.*

He looked at her now, but didn't see that emotion in her eyes anymore. It was all business, which was for the best.

This was better.

Was it?

"Why don't you have a seat and we'll go over some of the expectations," she said, motioning for him to take the empty seat in front of her desk.

"Sure." He sat down stiffly, uneasy about the tension that had descended between them. They were strangers, but weren't.

He was surprised to find how much it pained him that she was acting so distant, when they had once been so close.

You haven't been home in years. What did you expect?

It still bothered him to this day he couldn't have been here when they buried Logan, but he'd been stuck in the military hospital in Germany. Afterward there had seemed no point in coming back to a Jasper—Logan was gone and Candice was married—so he'd moved to Toronto.

He couldn't blame Candice for being mad at him, or even hating him. He had broken her heart and not been here for her when she needed him after losing her brother.

Candice flipped open his file. "So, you did your paramedic training with the Canadian military?"

"Yes. I was a medic and have my certification in wilderness medicine and surgery. I can perform minor surgeries in some of the roughest conditions."

"What kind of surgeries?" she asked.

"Sutures, removing shrapnel and tracheostomy. I've done a few chest tubes." Not that any of his skills had been useful when it had come to helping Logan in that crucial moment on the front lines…

"Hold on, buddy!" Jimmy had shouted above the gunfire.

They were slightly protected by the overturned truck, but a wall had crushed Logan's lower half and pinned both of Jimmy's legs, making it so he couldn't do anything to help Logan.

"I can't feel anything," Logan whispered. *"I think my pelvis and my spine are crushed. Pretty sure my femoral artery is severed."*

"You need to hold on. We're going to get you evacuated and into surgery."

Logan shook his head slowly. *"Promise me one thing."*

"Anything," Jimmy said.

"Take care of Candy for me."

"You can take of Candy yourself when you get home," Jimmy told him.

Logan had shaken his head again. *"I can't. I know I said keep away from her, but you have to promise me you'll look out for her. Promise me. I know she cares for you…"*

But he hadn't done that. He'd let her be, hoping she was happy.

The only reason he'd come home for the first time in four years was because he was looking for a way to make things right for his son.

Her eyebrows arched and she nodded. "That's impressive."

"Thank you."

"I can see why Head Office hired you." She closed his file.

"Thanks."

"We're headed into another busy season. The summer brings a lot of tourists to Jasper—as you're well aware—and the backcountry camping is now open, as well as the regular campsites. Most of these areas are patrolled by the park rangers, but we do have to help on some of the backcountry hikes."

"Okay," he said.

"A lot of visitors are unfamiliar with how fast the weather can change in the mountain, so it will help that you're a local, even if you haven't been back in…what, ten years?"

He wasn't going to let on he had been here four years ago. That he'd come back because of her, only to leave heartbroken.

"Yeah. Ten years," he said dryly.

She cocked her head to the side. "You okay? You seem to be in shock."

"I am a bit," he laughed nervously.

"Why?" she asked, folding her hands in front of her.

"To be honest, I didn't think that you would be running the mountain-rescue program in Jasper."

"Why?" she asked, those brown eyes narrowing again.

"You always wanted to go to medical school. I thought you'd be a surgeon or something by now."

A strange expression crossed her face, one he couldn't read, but it was obvious by the way she straightened her back that he'd touched a nerve, even though he hadn't meant to.

"Yes, well, circumstances change," she said stiffly. "After Logan died, my mother didn't take it so well and she passed away the following year. It was just me and my dad until last year, when I lost him to cancer. There's no time for medical school when you're trying to hold your family together."

It felt like Jimmy's stomach had dropped through the soles of his feet into the floor. He had heard that Logan's mom was gone, but he hadn't heard that Mr. Warner had passed, too. His parents hadn't told him that. The Warners had always been so kind to him, so welcoming. It was hard to believe they were gone.

"I—I don't know what to say, Candice. I'm so sorry." He meant it.

A half smile appeared on her lips, but didn't extend to her eyes. It was perfunctory. "I appreciate that."

She stood up and he followed, but was still shocked at how calm she'd been sharing just how much she'd lost since Logan had died— her mother, her father, her husband… She was completely alone.

She's your boss.

Candice held out her hand. "Welcome to Mountain Rescue."

Jimmy stared at her outstretched hand. What he wanted to do was give her a hug. Wanted to let her know that he was here for her. That he still cared for her. He wanted to hug her and comfort her, like he used to do. Like he always dreamed of doing every day he was away from her. Only, he couldn't do that. He'd broken her heart and he'd been gone so long that they were effectively strangers.

He took her small, delicate hand in his, reveling in the feel of her soft skin and hoping his palms weren't sweaty as they shook.

"I look forward to working with you." He held her hand longer than he intended and she pulled it away, a pink flush rising in her cheeks, which made his heart beat a bit faster.

"Samantha will show you where your gear is and will give you a temporary uniform…" She trailed off as the phone began to buzz. She answered it and sat down, grabbing a pen and paper to write down the details.

Jimmy stood quietly, unsure of what to do. Or where to go.

"Thanks, we'll be there soon." Candice hung up the phone and glanced at Jimmy. "I would get your gear together and change. Looks like your first assignment is right now. There's an injured hiker in Maligne Canyon, slipped down a ravine. We need to retrieve him. You up for this?"

Jimmy nodded, shaking away all those old thoughts, the sadness—everything that was swirling around his head. "I'm ready."

Candice smiled and nodded. "Then have Samantha show you where to get ready and we'll get on the move ASAP."

Jimmy nodded and opened the door, glancing back at Candice, who was on the phone again. He couldn't quite believe that they would be working together.

Little Candy Warner was his boss.

It's Lavoie now.

She was no longer that girl he had loved. His first love.

He couldn't afford to mess up this job. He

needed it to make a life for him and his son. He had to start over, even if it meant he was right back at the beginning again.

CHAPTER TWO

CANDICE DIDN'T KNOW WHY she was so nervous. She'd executed rescues at Maligne Canyon many times, but this was the first time she was doing it with Jimmy by her side.

Even though she was trying to tell herself she was over him, it was clear he was still affecting her. Making her nervous, making her fidget. She usually had good control over her emotions, but they had been all over the place since she'd first seen his name in that file.

She climbed into the back of the ambulance rig so that she could sit next to him. Another member of her team was driving and there was another truck with more gear following—essentials like climbing gear, water, blankets. Whatever they might need.

She didn't normally sit in the back, but Jimmy was new and usually the new employees stuck to her like glue during their first few missions. As much as she wanted to keep her distance from Jimmy right now, she couldn't. He was new and it was her responsibility to train him.

Her team was one of the best in the province and she wasn't going to mar that reputation by letting Jimmy go off on his own the first day. Just because she was uncomfortable being close to him didn't mean she wasn't going to do her job. Things had changed. Mountain Rescue's reputation under her command was all that mattered.

Her feelings did not.

"Where are we headed to, boss?" Stu asked from the front seat.

"Maligne Canyon. We need to park close to the first bridge lookout."

"Sounds good," Stu said.

Candice settled beside Jimmy as the siren sounded and they started on the highway toward Maligne Canyon, twenty minutes northeast of Jasper.

It was awkward sitting this close to him. Usually, it didn't bother her to be crammed in the back of the ambulance with her coworkers, but this was different.

This coworker had seen her naked.

"Did you find everything you needed?" she asked, clearing her throat.

"Yeah, I think so," he replied, going through his rucksack.

She noticed some medical gear she hadn't seen before. It looked like a surgical kit, but she wasn't sure.

"What's that?" she asked, leaning over.

"It's a kit I carry with my own gear. Something I suggested to head office."

Candice was impressed. "Well, we'll make sure you get what you need. Perhaps you can go over the kit with the group?"

"Sure." He went back to organizing his gear.

He was wearing a short-sleeve shirt and she silently admired his muscular forearms and the tattoo she didn't remember him having before. It was a simple geometric mountain with a lone spruce. It wasn't overly large, but she liked it quite a bit.

When they were teenagers, they all had talked about getting tattoos. Jimmy knew it would bother his overly strict parents, but he never went through with it in Jasper. Even when Logan had gotten one.

Even when she had gotten one. One she'd thought about getting rid of from time to time.

"Your tattoo is so sexy," he'd murmured when he'd first seen it, tracing the outline of it on her thigh with his finger.

"It's nothing huge," she said, his touch making her blood heat.

"It's a big deal to me, and that I'm the first you've shown it to."

He'd pulled her close in that tent and kissed her again.

She shook away that thought, annoyed that all these memories she'd thought were locked up were sneaking back in and distracting her.

Don't let him get in your head.

"Do you have bear spray in there?" she asked, trying not to let her thoughts overtake her.

"Ah, no. I think I forgot that." He frowned.

She pulled out a can from her bag. "Here, the bears are busy eating right now after their hibernation, so you never know what you'll come across. It's better to have it."

Jimmy smiled. "Thanks, boss."

It was so bizarre hearing him call her *boss*, instead of Candy.

You told him not to call you Candy. Remember? And everyone else calls you boss or by your last name.

It was just… She wasn't used to *Jimmy* calling her that.

Candice smiled. "You're welcome."

She swayed as the rig rocked and sped along the highway. The RCMP had shut down Maligne Lake Road and the parking lot close to bridge number one, where the hiker had fallen. If it was the spot that she was thinking of, it was a vertical drop down the side of the canyon and they would have to use their rappelling lines to hoist out the hiker.

She only hoped the hiker wasn't too badly injured or hadn't been washed away by the river.

"Do you remember how to rappel?" she asked.

"What?" Jimmy asked, his confusion evident as he looked up from his rucksack, obviously not having heard what she'd said.

"You and Logan used to do a lot of rock climbing and I'm wondering if you remember how to rappel down a rock face?"

He nodded. "I do. I kept it up when I was living in Toronto."

"Good, because if I'm right, the hiker is at the bottom of a pretty steep vertical drop. It'll be slick and the water will be cold. It will be a technically challenging retrieval."

"I'm ready," Jimmy stated firmly. "And I'm familiar with the area."

Candice smiled. "I know you are."

She didn't know what made her say that, because it had been so long since she'd seen him and she'd never witnessed him in an emergency situation. What made her think that he was ready?

Jimmy was a stranger, for all intents and purposes.

He's not a stranger.

She knew Jimmy Liu. A little too well.

Yes, she might be worried about working with Jimmy because of everything that had happened between them in the past, but she had no doubt that he was capable and that he would be an asset to the team. He came with glowing reports from his commanding officers.

She did have a niggling worry, though. Would he take orders from her?

Would he respect her?

If he respected you, he wouldn't have left the way he did.

She was annoyed for thinking that and for doubting herself. She was the head of Mountain Rescue, a first responder, a certified ranger and a pilot. He *would* do what she said.

What she needed to do was stop worrying unnecessarily and focus on the rescue.

That was all that mattered.

The ambulance slowed down and made a right turn onto Maligne Lake Road. They would be at the site soon.

"I can't believe someone climbed over the

fence," Jimmy murmured as they arrived at the trailhead.

"People do it a lot, unfortunately, to the point that it's a common rescue—though not always a positive outcome, One wrong move and the river can wash you away."

Jimmy nodded. "I'm willing to learn from you, boss."

Warmth spread through her. Maybe this wouldn't be as bad as she thought.

As the ambulance parked, they grabbed their gear, and Candice led the way to bridge number one. She just hoped that they would be able to get to the hiker easily.

Constable Bruce was waiting to speak to her and she motioned for Jimmy to follow her. Constable Bruce was one of the Mounties she liked dealing with the most. He knew his job well and was easy to work with. Some of the other, older Mounties still remembered her as a kid and didn't treat her with the same respect. Bruce had transferred from Toronto to Jasper and didn't have that shared history, so he treated her like a colleague should.

"Lavoie, I'm glad you're here," Constable Bruce said as she approached.

"Where else would I be?" Candice joked.

He smiled and then his gaze fell on Jimmy. "Ah, your team has a new paramedic, I hope?"

"Yes." Candice turned to Jimmy. "Jimmy Liu, this is Constable Bruce from the Jasper detachment. Jimmy served with the Canadian Armed Forces overseas. He has extensive experience working in harsh conditions."

Bruce raised his eyebrows, impressed. "Pleasure to meet you, Liu."

"Pleasure is all mine, Constable." Jimmy shook Bruce's hand.

"Well, the hiker climbed over the fence near the falls, right at the end of the trails. He was going to rappel down the limestone cliff to the bottom, but was unfamiliar with the porous limestone and his spike didn't hold," Bruce said.

Candice sighed. "Do you know how badly he's hurt?"

Bruce shook his head. "No. He did call out for help, but we haven't been able to communicate with him since his initial distress signal. His partner here tried to stop him—he's the one who called us—and he says the victim was acting strangely."

"Strangely?" Candice asked, alarm bells going off.

"I'll let you speak to his partner."

Candice and Jimmy exchanged glances. She was trying to piece together all the information she had to figure out what might have propelled the hiker to try and rappel down the side of the canyon.

Bruce led them over to the victim's worried-looking partner.

"Dean, this is our first responder Lavoie," Bruce said, introducing them. "Can you fill her in on what happened?"

Dean nodded, still obviously flustered. "Well, we had been up Roche Bonhomme. We decided to take the trail quite quickly because Reggie's training for an Ironman competition and he thought that elevating quickly and descending just as fast would help with his cardio endurance."

Candice groaned inwardly at that decision. It did not improve endurance if you weren't used to it.

"Are you from around here?" she asked.

Dean shook his head. "No, we're from Ontario. Reggie wanted to train in the mountains, for some reason. We've been in Jasper a couple of days and have been hitting the trails hard. I don't know what happened on the descent, but he started complaining of nausea and seemed off balance."

"Off balance?" Candice asked, her mind running through scenarios, putting the pieces together.

Ontario was closer to sea level than they

were. It could be altitude sickness or something more sinister, like a high-altitude pulmonary edema or a high-altitude cerebral edema.

"Yeah," Dean continued. "He was stumbling and then he wanted to climb over and rappel down the canyon. I was trying to convince him not to do that, but it was like he was drunk and there was nothing I can do to stop him. I tried to make sure his line was secure at the very least, but he moved so quick and the line gave way."

Candice nodded. "Thank you, Dean. I know this is stressful but I promise you we'll do our best to help Reggie."

She motioned for the team to follow her and they made their way along the well-marked trail to the viewing platform at the very end. She shivered as a cold gust of wind blew a mist of glacial water from the waterfalls below over her face.

Taking a deep breath, she steeled her resolve. "Let's get going."

Jimmy fell into step beside her. "What're you thinking?" he asked.

"Why don't you tell me your thoughts based on the info we have."

"A test?" he asked, cocking his eyebrow.

"Yes."

"I think acute mountain sickness, or AMS,

based on the irrational behavior and their recent climb."

"Impressive. AMS would explain what drove him to act irrationally. If it's an edema, he'll probably need a hyperbaric chamber and there's also whatever injuries he might have."

The rangers had come and cut the fence so her team would have access to rappel and get a backboard down. She was secretly pleased when Jimmy went straight to work getting his harness and his gear on. She didn't have to explain anything to him, so she could focus on getting ready to head down.

She was going to go down first and assess the situation and then Jimmy would follow.

It was a tricky descent, but she'd done retrievals at the bottom of this canyon before. Some were easy and some hadn't ended well, but she knew this rappel like the back of her hand.

Her only hope was that Reggie was at the bottom on a stable rock ledge and not in the water.

Candice focused on setting up her gear, and as she arranged her harness, Jimmy came up beside her and helped without her asking, or having to tell him what to do.

His hands around her as he pulled on her harness made her move just a bit faster. He was so close she could smell him. It made her skin break out in gooseflesh and she was glad she was wearing a long-sleeve shirt, so he couldn't see how he was affecting her.

"You're secure and I'll secure your line down. You don't want to make the same mistake the hiker did," Jimmy stated. "Limestone won't hold anything."

"I know," Candice said, unable to help herself from staring at him.

He smiled. "What? Why are you looking at me like you're surprised I know what I'm doing?"

Heat bloomed in her cheeks. "I'm not. It's just…"

"You forget I lived here my whole life. I know what kind of accidents can happen in the mountains, too."

"Yeah, but you haven't been home in a long time."

A strange expression crossed his face, and he turned away.

The rest of the team got into place and Jimmy helped to hold her line as she made her way to the edge with her pack. She did know this drop well, but as she stood at the edge and looked down, she still got that feeling in the pit of her stomach.

The one of exhilaration mixed with fear.

Her pulse drowned out the roar of the water tumbling down below her. She knew how damn cold that water was and she really didn't feel like taking a dip. All it took was one wrong move. The elements could shift something. Something might move.

It was nature and it was unpredictable.

Candice took a deep breath and pulled on her rucksack.

"Ready, boss!" Stu shouted from where he was standing next to Jimmy, who was preparing to go down next.

Candice nodded and, looking through the foliage, she scoped out where she wanted to land. She would slowly make her way down, and she just had to hope that she would be able to quickly spot Reggie, and that she had room to safely land at the bottom.

The water had shaped the soft rock in a gorgeously compelling way, but it wasn't exactly even and it definitely wasn't easy.

She made her way over the side and started her slow drop down the canyon wall. Her eyes focused on where she was going as she dangled in the air, slowly inching her way closer to the hiker, who was, thankfully, perched on a ledge.

The only sound she heard was the water. The ice-cold mist was spraying her back, but she was used to it and she'd learned to drown out the sensory overload and just focus on the task at hand. A life was at stake.

The farther she descended, the more her eyes adjusted to the dimness and she could better make out the victim, sprawled out on a rock ledge just inches from the rushing water.

"Reggie?" Candice called out. "Can you hear me?"

Reggie didn't respond, which meant that it was possible he was unconscious, and if he was unconscious it could mean a lot of different things. Her mind was racing as she ticked through everything it could be: internal bleeding, head trauma...

Her feet touched the canyon floor and she got her footing on the slippery rock, being mindful of the moss.

"I'm down," she called up. "Send Jimmy down!"

"Sure thing, boss!" Stu called back.

Candice set her rucksack down where she could access the medical supplies and it wouldn't be washed away.

She carefully made her way over to Reggie. His leg was bent at an odd angle, which probably meant a fracture. She couldn't see any blood, but that didn't mean he wasn't bleeding internally. Reggie was wearing a helmet, but she could see there was blood from a laceration on his face. That was superficial, but he could've also done something to his neck. She didn't know what was underneath him, other than rocks, or whether he'd hit his head on his way down.

A couple of rocks cascaded down the wall and she glanced up to see Jimmy making his descent.

She would be glad when he got down here and the two of them could properly assess Reggie, then get him on the backboard, which would follow Jimmy down.

She worried her bottom lip, watching Jimmy get closer, but it became apparent that she had nothing to worry about. Jimmy knew what he was doing.

After he joined her, they waited as the backboard was lowered down, and then Jimmy did an assessment of the patient's ABCs.

"Pupils are reactive, so that's a good sign," Jimmy muttered.

"He has a fracture in his leg," Candice stated. "We'll have to get that stabilized before we get him on the backboard and out of here."

Jimmy nodded and moved to Reggie's leg, palpating it, and frowned. "It's his femur, so there could be internal bleeding. I'm going to start an IV line of fluids and we need to get up him out of here. He needs oxygen now if we think this might be related to altitude sickness."

Candice nodded. "His fingernails are turning blue."

Jimmy frowned. "Yeah, he needs oxygen treatment."

They set about quickly setting up the IV lines and getting Reggie oxygen. Jimmy stabilized the leg and together they got him onto the backboard and covered him, then secured all his lines and made sure everything was strapped down.

Candice couldn't believe how seamlessly they worked together in the damp conditions down by the edge of a glacier-fed waterfall. It was surreal to see that the boy she'd known from childhood was now a strong, capable man, helping her save someone's life.

And he was doing a damn fine job.

"Pass me that line," he said.

"Sure." She reached across, their fingers brushing.

"I think everything is secure enough to move him," he said.

"Good. Let's get him out of here." She stood and together they lifted the backboard to secure it to the ropes, so Stu and the RCMP officers waiting at the top could pitch in to help get the backboard up the side of the cliff.

"You should go up with, Reggie," Candice said as they continued to hook up the harnesses and make sure that Reggie was stable. "You're the paramedic."

Jimmy nodded. "Okay, boss."

Candice had to help hook Jimmy's harness, and even though she'd done a vertical rescue like this before and had hooked up people on her team to a backboard many times over, having to hook up Jimmy was giving her pause.

Her pulse was thundering between her ears, and she only hoped that he didn't notice that her hands were trembling as she pulled the hooks and tethers across his chest.

Holy cow, he's more muscular than I remember.

She chastised herself for thinking like that as her cheeks heated. She knew that Jimmy was looking at her.

"You okay, boss?" he asked.

She cleared her throat and stepped behind him, tugging on a line. "Fine."

Only she wasn't fine.

What was this hold that Jimmy Liu had on her? She'd thought she'd gotten over this years ago, when he'd left and broken her heart.

She'd cried for weeks and then had found out she was pregnant with Jimmy's child.

She'd steeled herself to be a mother—to go

it alone—but just as she'd started to get truly excited, she'd lost the baby. And her heart had broken all over again.

So she'd closed off her heart as a means of getting through—the only way she could function and survive.

She thought she'd moved on, but being here with him, so close to him, touching him, brought it all back and it made her feel like that meek, quiet young woman again. It made her think of all her broken dreams, everything she'd lost.

Get a hold of yourself.

"You're good to go." She stepped back and pulled out her radio. "Stu, Jimmy's good to go and the patient is secure."

"Right," Stu responded.

Over the roar of the waterfall, she could hear the team at the top, and slowly Jimmy began to ascend the side of the cliff, keeping the backboard stable.

Candice took a deep breath and watched from below, holding the ropes from the bottom and doing her part to make sure that the patient got to the top of the cliff safely.

Once they were to the top and Jimmy was over the side, she slipped on her rucksack and made the ascension herself.

Her climb up was quicker than Jimmy's and

when she got to the top the rest of her team were already heading toward the helicopter that would airlift Reggie to the hospital. The helicopter had landed on the main road, because there wasn't much room in the small parking lot.

Jimmy helped unhook her and she took off her helmet, then made her way to the air ambulance. Stu was going to accompany Reggie to the hospital as he was a paramedic and Jimmy didn't have the clearance yet, so Jimmy briefed him on his initial observations.

"Stu, the patient has a suspected broken femur. An obvious laceration to the head, but pupils were reactive. There didn't appear to be any blunt trauma, though the patient did fall, but I'm suspecting AMS. Possibly a high altitude pulmonary edema or a high altitude cerebral edema. The patient is from Ontario and his partner was reporting strange behavior associated with AMS. He was also slightly cyanotic."

Stu nodded. "I'll monitor his oxygen."

Candice helped load the patient on the helicopter and then stepped away, ducking as the helicopter's blades began to whir. She blocked her face from the dust being kicked up and watched as the helicopter rose from the highway and took off toward the hospital.

As the helicopter disappeared in the distance, she saw that Jimmy was giving instructions to Dean and the RCMP was waiting to accompany Reggie's distraught partner.

Candice took a deep breath.

The rescue had gone well, even if Jimmy brought out all those unexpected and unwanted emotions in her.

Emotions she thought had been long buried.

She was annoyed with herself for letting her control slip like that, but she had to learn to deal with it. Jimmy didn't want her back. He'd made it clear when he left, breaking her heart after she'd offered it up to him.

And that was fine.

She had found love after him.

Yeah, and look how that turned out. You're divorced and he wasn't exactly the catch you thought.

Chad had left her when she needed him most.

Just like Jimmy.

Candice shook away that thought. The point was, she'd grown up since Jimmy Liu left Jasper. She'd mourned her brother alone, taken care of her parents.

She'd outgrown her foolish crush on Jimmy and she had to keep reminding herself of that. Except, when she looked at him, it was like no time had passed. Sure, things had changed, but he just brought her back to those happy days together before it all ended.

It was the last time she'd felt truly happy. Logan and her parents had still been alive and she'd thought Jimmy was the one.

You're fooling no one.

"Everything okay?" Candice asked as Jimmy made his way over to her.

"Yeah. The RCMP will take care of Dean."

"We'll have to get you hospital clearance so you can accompany the patients in future. It should've been you riding in that helicopter instead of Stu."

A strange look passed over his face. Almost like fear, but it was a brief and his expression relaxed, though the smile didn't extend to his eyes. It was forced, like he was trying to hide something. "Right. Sure."

"You sure you're okay?" she asked, puzzled by his behavior.

"Not a huge fan of helicopters or planes, if I'm honest. Don't like flying. Reminds me of…" His lips pursed together as he paused. "Doesn't matter."

She had a feeling that it did matter, but it wasn't her business. When Jimmy had left her, she'd closed her heart to him. The only thing that should concern her about Jimmy now was

AMY RUTTAN
53

how he fit in at Mountain Rescue and how he did his job. That's all that mattered.

Nothing else.

A lot had changed in ten years. They both were different people.

She was a different person.

Are you?

If she was going to make this situation work, then she had to keep her distance from Jimmy Liu.

"Well, we better get back to Jasper. I don't have my rig license, but we can take the pickup and we'll go over your first rescue."

"Sure. Sounds good, boss." He avoided her gaze as he walked away to help pack up the rest of their gear.

Candice cursed herself. She should've made him ride in the rig. They had time to go over his first rescue later.

Having him ride with her in the pickup was not distancing herself from him.

She hated that he brought out this irrational side of her.

She hated that she went right back to being that unsure girl who'd lacked confidences.

The girl who had been in love with Jimmy Liu.

CHAPTER THREE

YOU'VE GOT TO get a hold of yourself, Jimmy.

He knew that working with Mountain Rescue would involve helicopters. He'd grown up watching them fly past, but since his time in the Middle East and that last mission he'd served there, helicopters had become something he feared—the cause of the explosion that had injured him and killed Logan.

He'd felt good about the rescue today until the helicopter had arrived—he was annoyed with himself, both for forgetting that a rescue like this usually required an air transport and for letting it get to him.

He thought he was over it.

How long had he worked with Kristen, his therapist, to get over his traumatic experiences overseas? Having seen Candice married and happy in Jasper four years ago, he'd wanted to better himself, so he'd started going to see Kristen when he was back in Toronto.

He needed help to move past the trauma of his injury.

Past the trauma of Logan's death.

The trauma of losing Candice.

It was a dark period of his life and he'd be the first to admit he'd lived recklessly for a while. But those years hadn't been all bad.

One good thing came out of it.

Marcus.

It's not exactly how he ever pictured his life turning out, but becoming a father had helped Jimmy start to heal the rift between him and his parents. Helped him to understand them in a new light, to experience the drive a parent feels to provide for their child, even if that means making hard decisions. Having Marcus had gotten his life back on track and brought Jimmy back to his family.

He would do whatever it took to continue to turn his life around for his son.

He needed to get control of his fear of helicopters. He couldn't even help load Reggie onto the helicopter, and when he'd watched Candice move with ease toward it, it had made him worry about her.

Made him panic.

Because it brought him straight back to the day Logan died. They'd been trying to evacuate, but the helicopter had been hit by a missile, exploding and sending them flying.

This is not a war zone. Candice is safe.

He thought he had better control. He hadn't had an episode like that in a long time.

At least it wasn't a full-blown panic attack on his first day. He was trying to make a good impression.

There was a thud, knocking those thoughts from his head, and the pickup slowed.

"Dammit," Candice cursed, as she flicked on her four-way flashers and brought the truck to a stop at a lookout on the shoulder of the highway, where the majestic sight of the Athabasca River and the peaks of Roche de Smet and Gargoyle Mountain could usually be viewed.

But you couldn't really make out the peaks in this mist and fog, so the lookout was empty. There wasn't even a mountain goat or an elk nearby to pique a tourist's interest and compel them to stop.

It was just them.

"Flat?" Jimmy asked as Candice cursed under her breath again.

"Yes." She groaned, shifting the truck into Park. She leaned her head against the steering wheel, banging it ever so lightly in frustration.

"Come on. Surely you know how to change

a flat. I mean, your brother and I showed you enough times."

She glared at him. "I'm quite capable of changing a flat tire."

"Then why the cursing?" he teased.

"It's the last thing I need. A flat tire with you in the truck."

He cocked an eyebrow. "What's that supposed to mean?"

She shook her head and mumbled again, undoing her seat belt and opening the door.

Jimmy was confused. He didn't know what he'd done, but this was not the Candice he remembered.

This Candice was stressed.

Unhappy.

Do you even know what happiness is? When was the last time you were happy?

Jimmy sighed and undid his seat belt, sliding out of the passenger side of the truck. He closed the door and made his way to the back, where Candice had pulled out her emergency roadside kit and was busy setting up cones around the perimeter of the truck.

"We're on an overlook. No one is going to hit us," he said offhandedly, watching her methodically place the cones.

"It's also foggy. The last thing we need is

some big recreational vehicle slamming into us out of the fog."

She had a point.

"Give me those," he said, taking the rest of the fluorescent cones and placing them around the front of the pickup.

After he finished, he asked, "Well, do you need me to replace the flat?"

"Nope." She said, standing there with her arms crossed.

"Okay. Then are you going to do it?" he asked, confused as to why she was just standing there.

"Nope."

Jimmy scratched his head. "Look, I'm no rocket scientist by any means, but one of us has got to change the tire if we want to get this truck moving again."

"We can't change a tire that isn't there."

"What do you mean it's not there?"

She held up her hands in exasperation. "The spare is not here."

Jimmy checked the flat tire and frowned, realizing what the problem was. "It is here, actually. It's just already on the truck."

"Great." Candice pulled out her phone and called for help. They would need a tow and a ride back to the station, because of the fog, the ambulance was way ahead of them now. She ended the call. "I guess all we can do now is wait."

"Did they say how long they were going to be?" he asked, glancing at his watch. He'd promised his parents that he wouldn't be late tonight picking up Marcus. He didn't want to wait hours by the side of the road.

Jimmy knew deep down that his parents wouldn't care if he was late because they adored Marcus and were so thrilled to be grandparents, but Marcus was going through a bit of a shy stage. When they lived in Toronto, he hadn't see his grandparents much, so he hadn't known them well when he and Jimmy had moved back to Jasper. Now they were here, Marcus was getting used to them, but still preferred having his dad close by.

"Why are you in such a rush?" Candice asked.

"I have to get home to my son," he said firmly, annoyed by the flat tire and the delay it was causing.

Candice's eyes widened. "Your—your son?"

"Yeah."

"I didn't know that you had a son," she said.

"I wouldn't think so," Jimmy teased. "This is the first time I've mentioned him, after all."

Candice crossed her arms and slowly walked

over to him. "So your wife is expecting you home?"

"My wife?" Jimmy chuckled and shook his head. "No. I'm not married. Marcus's mother is not in the picture."

Marcus's mom, Jennifer, had been a one-night stand.

Jimmy hadn't even known he was a father until Marcus was six months old—that was when Jennifer had left their son on his doorstep. For a long time he'd resented Jennifer for hiding her pregnancy. He hated that he hadn't been there when Marcus was born, but he was learning to let that go because now he had Marcus and his son was a gift.

"Where is Marcus's mom? Is she from Jasper?" Candice asked as she sat next to him on the guardrail.

"No. She was from Toronto. She served overseas, like me. It was just a one-time thing and about six months after Marcus was born she showed up and dropped him off, almost as though she was discarding him. She had a lot of PTSD issues and I tried to find her, to get her help, but before I could she was killed in an accident. So it's been just Marcus and me for the last year. I'd been trying to better myself for some time and Marcus's birth made me realize I had to do a lot more than I was," he said softly. "I was so angry that she didn't tell me she was pregnant—that I couldn't be there, you know?"

"Right," Candice said quickly, looking away.

He couldn't believe that he was admitting this to Candice. Obviously it was making her uncomfortable.

He hadn't even told his own parents everything that happened since he'd been discharged from the armed forces. How serving had messed him up so completely, the extent of his injuries overseas...

His parents were easily connecting with Marcus, but Jimmy still had a hard time opening up to them. They'd been so distant when he was growing up, always working, so focused on the hotel that it often felt like they'd forgotten they even had a son. He'd never been able to trust in them in the past, so it was difficult to do so now.

Difficult to trust anyone, really.

"I'm so sorry to hear about Marcus's mother. How old is your son?" Candice asked.

Jimmy smiled. "He'll be two in a couple of months. He's a handful."

"Who has him now?"

"My mom. She loves being a grandma."

Candice smiled at him, but there was a sadness in that smile. Something she wasn't saying.

"She's lucky. My mom would've loved being a grandma. I think she was hoping for that when I got married to my ex, but it was never meant to be."

"Why?" he asked.

Candice sighed. "Well, she died a year after I got married, but it wouldn't have happened even if she'd lived... Chad didn't want kids. He said he did in the beginning, but changed his mind after we were married for a couple of months."

"How long have you been divorced?"

"Three years. We were only married for two. We separated when my dad got sick because he wanted to go back to med school, but I couldn't leave my dad alone in Jasper."

"Sorry to hear it didn't work out."

Only, there was a part of him—a surprisingly large part—that wasn't sorry that it hadn't worked out. He looked at her, sitting next to him on the guardrail in the fog. Her dark hair was tied back, the same way she sometimes used to wear it, but she was a very different woman than the one he'd left behind. Not just because she was in a mountain-rescue uniform with big black boots instead of a flannel shirt, jeans with holes in the knees and Converse sneakers. There was so much more that had changed—he could see it in her eyes and hear it in her voice. So much more she was keeping from him now.

Instead of her head down and her dark hair hiding her face, she was looking straight ahead with determination, her arms crossed.

This wasn't the same girl he'd fallen in love with.

He glanced over his shoulder at the Athabasca River. It was moving swiftly, the summer melt making it swell, and this section of the river was so wide it almost seemed like a lake. This wasn't far from where they had camped that night—the night everything changed between them.

"Remember that time Logan went skinny-dipping just over there?" he asked, thinking of that moment when he'd had to bear witness to his best friend's bare ass.

A smile tugged at the corners of Candice's mouth. "I try not to. I mean, I wasn't exactly thrilled my big brother decided to strip off all his clothes in front of me and go skinny-dipping."

"He was drunk."

She forced a smile. "I remember. I painfully remember."

"Come on. It was funny."

"You weren't traumatized by it. You don't have siblings so you have no idea how gross it is when your brother gets naked in front of you." She scrubbed a hand over her face. "You two were always doing nonsense like that and dragging me along!"

"You didn't have to be dragged along. You seemed to go willingly."

A pink blush rose in her cheeks and she quickly looked at him, then averted her gaze. "Well...yeah, I didn't really have a lot of friends. Logan was my best friend, too."

"And what about me?"

The blush deepened and she glanced up at him. "What do you mean, 'what about me'?"

"Wasn't I your friend?"

What are you doing, man?

He wasn't sure what he was trying to do. He promised himself that he wasn't going to treat her with familiarity. She was his boss and she'd made it quite clear that there was nothing between them beyond a professional relationship.

But he found that when he was around her, he couldn't help himself. All those old feelings that he used to have for her came flooding back.

Even though he'd kept away from Jasper— from Candice—seeing her again proved that those feelings had never faded away. Just sitting here with her made his blood heat, his heart race. He reached out and touched her face. He could feel her tremble under his touch.

"No. I thought you were my friend, but you weren't."

She got up and walked away.

Jimmy was disappointed, but really, what could he expect? He's let her down in so many ways over the years.

He ran his hand through his hair.

"Yeah, I suppose I deserved that," he muttered.

She turned on her heel. "Deserved what?"

"Your rejection," he said. "I have a lot to apologize for."

She pursed her full lips together. "Yes, you do."

He stared at the ground, not entirely sure what to say.

She sighed. "Fine. You were my friend, too, I suppose, but you were a crappy friend."

He chuckled in relief that she was letting him off the hook…for now. "How so?"

"You let me see my brother's bare ass and did nothing to stop it." There was a twinkle in her eye. This was the Candice he remembered. She may have been shy, almost like a wallflower when they were young, but there were moments when she could take you down with a one-line zinger. It was one of the many things he'd always loved about her.

"Yeah, I guess that does make me a crappy friend." He hopped down from the guardrail and glanced back out over the water. He could make out Gargoyle Mountain through the mist. "We did drag you to a lot of places that you probably didn't want to go."

"Who said I didn't want to go?" she asked.

"Well, most girls that were your age at the time didn't want to go traipsing through the woods and drag racing and…whatever stupid things Logan and I used to do."

She smiled as she approached him. "I liked those stupid things you and Logan used to do. I never fit in with the other girls, anyway. I guess that's why boys never asked me out. I wasn't girly enough."

"I wouldn't say that," he said.

Candice looked up at him, the pink rising in her cheeks again. "What?"

"Guys liked you, Candy. You just didn't notice." He took a step closer to her and fought the urge to reach out and touch her face. To pull her in his arms and kiss her. "*I* liked you."

There was a flush of pink in her cheeks. "I liked you, too."

Get a hold of yourself.

Only, he couldn't.

All he could think about was that night by the river.

Jimmy's pulse was thundering in his ears as he moved closer to her.

"That night…"

"Don't," she whispered.

"Candice."

She bit her lip and he bent down, unable to resist her.

There was a honk and Jimmy took a step back, the spell of the moment broken as the tow truck came to rescue them.

"I better go…deal with the tow-truck driver," she said awkwardly, not looking at him.

"Yeah."

Candice walked away and Jimmy scrubbed his hand over his face, annoyed that he couldn't control himself around her. Even after all this time.

Candice stayed late to fill out paperwork. Once they'd gotten back to the station, she hadn't said a word to Jimmy, other than to help get him set up with some paperwork and an online training course. When their shift was done, he left, but she stayed behind.

She tried to focus on work, but all she could think about was the fact that they'd almost kissed and the revelation that he had a son.

It made her heart ache and brought back all the pain of losing their child. The one he never knew about.

You have to tell him.

She knew she did. But he'd mentioned how he was so angry that Marcus's mom hadn't told him about Marcus, so what would he think when she told him about their lost baby?

She was scared.

She was also scared at the effect he had on her.

Her body trembled as she thought of their near kiss.

She was glad that the tow truck had come just then.

Candice sighed. She got up from her desk and wandered to the window, looking out at the distant mountain range. There were a few bighorn sheep wandering in the parking lot, but everything else was quiet and calm.

Except her.

Seeing Jimmy had completely rattled her.

It brought back all these ghosts from her past. Ones that she thought were long gone. She'd been a fool to think that they were.

There was a knock at her door.

"Come in," she called.

Stu opened the door and stuck his head in. "Just got back from Edmonton."

"Oh, Reggie was transported to Edmonton?"
Stu nodded. "You were right."

"Right?" she asked, confused.

"About acute mountain sickness and in particular HAPE. He had a pulmonary edema and is in the hyperbaric chamber. He was given some dexamethasone. Reggie was going up peaks too quickly. His body hadn't adjusted to the altitude."

"Seems odd, though," Candice stated, letting the part of her that wanted to be a doctor sneak through.

"Why's that?" Stu asked, leaning against the door.

"He was in shape."

Stu nodded. "Seemed like it, eh?"

"What do you mean?"

"He wasn't really. His partner said he lost over one hundred pounds in less than a year. He had bariatric surgery. Reggie's heart was weak and couldn't handle what he was putting it through. If he trained for his big race somewhere else, then he could've slowly built his heart muscle up, improved his cardiovascular system. Instead he was here and he pushed himself too far."

"And paid the price," Candice sighed. "That's too bad. Just goes to show you that you can't judge a book by its cover."

Stu nodded. "He should be okay. You got oxygen to him in the nick of time. The emergency doctor praised you for that."

"It wasn't just me. It was our new paramedic, Jimmy, too."

Stu smiled. "Yeah, he seems like a good guy."

"He was…" She shook her head. "I mean he is."

"I'm going to head for home. You should, too, boss. You're still getting over that nasty flu. Don't push yourself too hard."

"Thanks, Stu. Good night."

Stu left, shutting the door. Candice sighed. She was glad that Reggie was going to be okay. And Jimmy had noticed the cyanosis before she did. She was thinking altitude sickness, but in that moment he'd caught the subtle blue tinge of Reggie's nail beds and they'd gotten him oxygen.

It was a job well done.

Jimmy had told her that she was too good to waste her life here and she had to admit that there were moments that she regretted that she didn't get to finish medical school. If she had, she'd be a doctor now, like Chad was, but she had stayed behind with her dad. Yes, her dad had insisted over and over that she return to school, but she couldn't bear to leave him.

So what's stopping you now?

Other than work, nothing was keeping her here. But she loved her job and it was days like this—having helped to save Reggie's life—that reminded her that hers was a life worth living.

But you're alone.

She couldn't deny that. She was alone.

It was in times like these she often wondered what her life would have been like if she hadn't lost their baby.

She'd have someone.

Dammit, Jimmy.

She groaned and shut down her computer, then grabbed her purse and jacket. She hadn't been questioning anything about her life when she woke up this morning, but then he came walking through her door.

An unwelcome ghost from her past.

Is he unwelcome, though?

She shook away that thought and clicked off the office light.

She needed to get home.

And she needed to put Jimmy Liu out of her mind.

This was her life and there was no room for ghosts.

CHAPTER FOUR

THE MOMENT SHE pulled into the driveway at home, Candice realized she didn't have anything to eat in the house and she really didn't feel like takeout.

Usually, she did her grocery shopping outside of Jasper, especially during tourist season, when the prices were a bit higher, but the thought of the hour-long drive to Hinton and getting food there wasn't appealing. So she sucked it up, changed, picked up a couple of reusable bags and walked the fifteen minutes downtown to the small grocery store.

Downtown Jasper had come alive. It was a beautiful summer evening and with the summer sun almost at its solstice, it was staying light out later in the evening.

Candice usually liked to avoid the tourist crowds because it got loud at night, which she hated, but tonight it was a welcome distraction.

It got her mind off of Jimmy.

"Hey, Candy!"

She turned around and there he was—Jimmy. And, in his arms, a little boy who looked an awful lot like him, except for the layer of chocolate ice cream around his mouth. He smiled at her with chubby cheeks, then rubbed his eyes, smearing more melted ice cream all over his face. Next he buried his face on Jimmy's shoulder, spreading the chocolate over his white T-shirt.

"Hey yourself," Candice chuckled as Jimmy glanced down at his once clean shirt and rolled his eyes.

"I didn't expect to run in to you here," he said.

Ditto.

"Yeah, well, I had errands to run and felt like a walk." Her eyes tracked back to the adorable boy clinging to his father.

It made her heart melt. It made her long for what could've been.

"So this is your son, I take it?" she asked, hoping her voice wasn't shaking.

"Yeah, this is Marcus and what remains of his chocolate ice-cream cone."

Marcus looked at her shyly from his father's shoulder.

"Hi, Marcus. How are you?" she asked brightly.

Marcus smiled, but still kept his head on his father's shoulder.

"This is Candy, Marcus. She's my boss and an old friend of Daddy's," Jimmy said. Marcus stared up at his father and then smeared chocolate on his cheek. "Thanks, buddy. I appreciate it."

Candice couldn't help but laugh. "It's a good look on you."

"Thanks," Jimmy said dryly. "Do you happen to have a tissue or something? My arms are a bit full."

"Sure." Candice pulled out a packet of wet wipes she carried in her purse and wiped off Jimmy's face. Then Marcus held out his chubby hands and stared at her intently. "You want clean hands?"

Marcus nodded and then giggled as she took his little hands in hers and wiped away the melted ice cream, first off his little fingers and then his adorable cheeks.

"Thanks," Jimmy said. "You really saved the day there."

"You're welcome. What're you doing downtown so late?"

"Well, I took Marcus to the park and then we had some ice cream, obviously, and then we were going to get some groceries for Năinai."

"I was heading to the grocery store, too," Candice said.

"Mind if we join you?" Jimmy asked.

Say no. Say no.

"Sure."

Jimmy fell into step beside her. Marcus was clearly tired, with his head still on his father's shoulder and his thumb in his mouth.

"He really is adorable," Candice said. She couldn't help but stare at Marcus. He was so cute. She never knew if her lost baby had been a boy or a girl, but she often thought it would have been a boy. "He's almost two?"

Jimmy nodded. "Yep. Almost two—right, buddy?"

Marcus nodded his head.

"Looks like the trip to the park wore him out. Although, that chocolate ice cream might wake him back up again later."

Jimmy chuckled softly and shifted Marcus to his other arm. "He played pretty hard. Where we lived in Toronto wasn't the greatest, so it wasn't always safe to play in the park. I made the right decision coming back home."

"I'm sure your mother was thrilled." Candice knew that though Jimmy and his parents had had their issues, Mr. and Mrs. Liu had missed him. He was their only child.

"My mother is over-the-moon happy. She

came to Toronto for a while when I found out I had a son and was given custody. I had no idea what to do with an infant, but my mom helped. That's when the nagging to come back to Jasper started. I had to get some stuff together before I could come back home, though."

"I bet your mom begged you to move into her place."

Jimmy laughed. "She did, but I rented a place down the street from your parents' old place, actually. It's a small modular home, but it's good for Marcus and me."

Her heart skipped a beat. "You... So you're my neighbor?"

"You're still at your parents' place?"

"It's my place now, since Dad died."

His expression softened. "Right. Sorry."

"No, it's fine." They walked into the grocery store.

Candice got Jimmy a cart and Marcus whined a bit as Jimmy sat him down in it, but soon was happy when Jimmy began to push the cart around the store.

Jimmy pulled out his list. "Thankfully her list is small and once I get that car seat installed she can make trips into Hinton with Marcus."

"Yeah, it's cheaper to drive out there to the

co-op rather than hit the small grocery store, especially with all the tourists."

"Where the heck would nutmeg be?" Jimmy asked, staring at the list and scratching his head. "And what the heck is nutmeg?"

Candice shook her head. "Come on. We'll share the cart and I'll help you."

"Yeah, but that still doesn't answer the question of what a nutmeg is."

"It's not a thing, it's a spice," Candice teased. "Come on. Seriously, how did you survive on your own in Toronto?"

"Takeout," he muttered, picking up a bunch of bananas.

Candice snickered and Marcus smiled up at her. She couldn't help but smile back down at him. Not only was he cute, but he also had the biggest, brightest smile. He had that charm that his father had.

And Candice felt her heart melt when she looked down at the chubby little toddler.

It made her long for their lost baby. A lump formed in her throat and she tried not to think about it. Although it was hard. Marcus reminded her of the thing she longed for the most.

Family.

"So, Stu came back from Edmonton and

Reggie is stable," she said, trying to distract herself from being around Jimmy and Marcus.

"That's great to hear," Jimmy said. "Did he have AMS?"

Candice nodded, then picked up a canister of nutmeg and handed it to Jimmy, who examined the bottle, wrinkling his nose as he put it in his cart.

"What do you use this for?" he asked. "It smells strong."

"Baking."

"Bleh." Jimmy shook his head and they continued their meander down the aisle. "What about HAPE or HACE?"

"Pulmonary edema."

"Huh, but he was athletic."

"Ah, it appeared so, but Reggie had lost a lot of weight too fast. Like, over a hundred pounds in less than a year and he hadn't been working too long on improving his cardiovascular health before he went gung ho up the trails."

"Ah, that makes a lot of sense. You've got to acclimatize slowly if you're not in the best of health. People think losing weight fast automatically makes them healthy, but it doesn't. You have to build muscle, too."

"He should be okay."

"Glad to hear it. I guess that explains why

he went a bit crazy and decided to repel down Maligne Canyon," Jimmy said.

"You can't always blame AMS on that," she said offhandedly, adding her stuff to their shared cart. "Even people not suffering AMS do that."

"Yeah, but then it's just stupidity."

She snorted. "Welcome to Mountain Rescue."

Jimmy smiled at her and there was that twinkle in his eye. The one that made her weak in the knees. It was so easy to talk to him.

It was easy to be around him in general.

You can be friends with him. You were once before.

"I'm glad to be a part of Mountain Rescue. I'm glad I was able to do what the armed forces trained me to do and that I can do it back in my old hometown."

She couldn't help but think of that night down by the river, when he said that he had to get out of Jasper. That there was nothing for him in this town.

Now he was thankful to be back.

"Maybe you've finally seen the error of your ways then?" she asked.

"What do you mean?" he asked.

"You told me once that there was nothing here."

He looked confused. "Did I?"

"You did."

"When?"

"Right before you and Logan left for basic training. The night we…" She trailed off, not wanting to say it.

"Right," he said, clearing this throat and looking away. "I've realized I was a complete idiot back then."

"That you were," Candice muttered as she walked away from him, into the next aisle.

They finished up their grocery shopping and Candice walked with Jimmy to the downtown parking lot, helping load his groceries in his trunk while he buckled Marcus into his car seat. The little boy had drifted off to sleep on the walk.

"Do you want a ride home? I mean, we are practically neighbors."

"Thanks," she said. "I'm okay."

"It's getting pretty dark," he said. "It's no trouble. Marcus sleeps well in the car. Let me drive you home."

She worried her bottom lip. She should really just say no, but she did buy ice cream and the longer she stood here, it became less ice and more cream.

"Sure. Thanks." She climbed into the passenger seat.

Jimmy go into the vehicle and slowly pulled out of the parking lot. "Now, to remember how to get out of this downtown area."

"Turn right at the end of the street and follow it up to the edge of town."

It was only a five-minute drive from the bustling downtown to the western-most edge of Jasper and her parents' little log-and-stone home that backed into the forest and the vast wilderness of Jasper National Park.

Jimmy pulled into the driveway, behind her SUV.

"Thanks for the ride."

He nodded. "Anytime. I'll see you at work tomorrow."

She nodded. "Yes. We have some training to do up the mountain."

"I look forward to it."

"I wouldn't," she teased.

Candice got out of the car and quickly made her way up the driveway. She didn't look back. She didn't want to look back.

They could be friends, but nothing more. Even if he *was* stirring up all these old feelings inside her. She wasn't willing to put her heart at risk again.

She'd find the courage to tell him about the loss of their baby and then she would keep her distance from him.

* * *

Jimmy sat in Candice's driveway for a few minutes, making sure that she got in okay. It was a bit surreal to be back in front of the old Warner place. He'd spent many happy times here with Logan, with Candice.

The little log home made of wood and stone was something he thought about often. He thought about all the times he and Logan would hike through the small woodlot behind the house, down to the little spring.

How you could see Whistlers Peak and the tiny station at the top, where the tourists could ride a gondola up to see Jasper from on high.

How many times had they sat on the porch at night in the summer or played basketball at the end of the long drive?

It was kind of hard to believe that the Warners were gone.

And that Candice was alone.

He should've never left—he'd been a fool.

He should've stayed in Jasper. He could've become a paramedic and stayed with Candice.

You would've held her back.

And if he had stayed, he wouldn't have had those last moments with Logan.

He wouldn't have Marcus.

He glanced in the rearview mirror to watch

Marcus sleeping and he couldn't help but smile at him.

The light came on in Candy's front room and he slowly pulled out of her drive and headed back to his parents' place on the other side of town to deliver his mom's groceries. They lived in a small wartime home near the hotel district. His parents had run a small motel, but had sold it off and were now retired.

His mom wanted him to move back home, but for their newfound good relationship to remain the way it was, it was better for Jimmy and Marcus to live on their own.

His mother met him at the car.

"You're late," she said.

"Sorry. I ran in to Candy Warner and she was walking home with her groceries, so I offered her a ride."

His mother gave him a quick smile, but then it disappeared. "Oh. That was nice of you."

"She's also my boss. And I guess she's not actually Candy Warner now. She's Candice Lavoie."

"Yes, but she's divorced," his mother remarked, opening the back door of the car and slowly taking out a bag of groceries, so as to not wake up Marcus.

Jimmy cocked an eyebrow. "That doesn't change the fact she's my boss."

"I know, but you're the one who mentioned her name change."

"Mom, did you know that Candice was going to be my boss?" he asked.

Her eyes widened and she blinked a couple of times. "Of course."

"Why didn't you tell me? You could've warned me."

"What was there to tell? You were friends with her and Logan. I didn't think it would matter." Her mother narrowed her eyes. "Does it matter?"

Yeah.

Only he couldn't say that out loud. His mom didn't know what had happened between him and Candice ten years ago. And though she didn't need to know, it did matter that Candice was his boss.

If he'd known she was going to be his boss… he would've gone in more prepared. He still would've taken the job, but he would've been prepared. He hadn't been prepared to see her.

He had to learn to deal with seeing her. Just like he had to deal with helicopters being used for mountain rescues.

He had to deal with it all, because nothing was going to change.

Candice was off-limits and helicopters were part of his job.

Great. Now you're comparing Candice to helicopters. You need to get a grip.

"Nope."

"Good. Did you get everything on the list?" his mother asked as she walked up the drive and he followed behind carrying the rest of her bags.

"Yes."

"And why is my grandson so sticky?" she asked.

"Ice cream."

His mother made a face and disappeared inside.

Jimmy sighed and dropped the rest of the bags just inside the door. He glanced up at the half moon in the dark sky. It was twilight and soon it would be dark enough to see the stars.

The thought of seeing stars made him think of Candice and that night by the river, and of Candice all alone now, just down the street from him.

But there was nothing he could do about it.

With his son, with his traumatic past, he would hold her back. Just like Logan always said he would.

She was free.

He was not.

CHAPTER FIVE

JIMMY WAS SITTING on the grass with the rest of the Mountain Rescue crew, having just hiked up the Overlander trail. They were supposed to wait for Candice to show up, but Jimmy was confused as to how she was to get there, because was no way to access the meadow with a vehicle.

He had a horrible feeling that she was probably coming by helicopter, so he was bracing himself for that. He had to control his panic, so he wouldn't lose trust with his teammates.

"Is she always this late?" Jimmy asked Stu.

"Sometimes. Depends if she can get her flight plan approved or whether there's cloud cover by the airport."

"Her flight plan?" Jimmy asked, his heart skipping a beat as he sat upright. "She flies?"

Stu nodded. "Yep. Not always, but she does. I think Nigel is flying the helicopter today, though. He's relatively new, as well, but he's been around for four months."

Jimmy couldn't believe what he was hearing.

Candice was a helicopter pilot.

A ball of dread formed in the pit of his stomach. The idea of Candice in a helicopter was a bit too much to bear. The thought of her getting hurt made his stomach churn and twist.

"Here comes Nigel now. I bet Lavoie is with him," Stu said offhandedly as he got up off the ground.

Jimmy was frozen.

He closed his eyes and tried to remember all the tricks that Kristen had taught him to deal with the panic that was currently rising in him.

He told himself that he was standing in a meadow off the Overlander trail—a trail that he hiked all the time with Logan when they were kids.

That he wasn't back overseas…

"Get under cover!" Logan had shouted over the gunfire.

Jimmy made his way to the helicopter, but before the helicopter had a chance to land, it exploded in a fireball and he was thrown back.

More explosions thundered through the air and he covered his head.

But not before he'd seen the crumbling wall coming toward him and Logan...

Jimmy shook the nightmare away as the propellers died down. Candice climbed out of the helicopter and he shook the remnants of the memory from his mind. He had a job to do and Candice was his boss. He had to prove to her he had what it took to do this work.

Candice was handing Stu gear from the helicopter.

He was on edge—the anxiety wasn't abating—but he swallowed his fear and made his way to the helicopter.

"Look alive," Candice said, tossing him a bag.

He caught it and walked away from the helicopter, then put down the bag where Stu was setting up equipment with Kate.

He needed to shake this anxiety.

He needed to focus on his work, but he was struggling.

"You okay, Jimmy?" Candice asked, coming up beside him.

"Fine," he said sternly.

She cocked her head to the side and he knew just from her expression she didn't believe him, but he didn't care. It wasn't really any of her business. Just like it wasn't his business if she wanted to be a fool and fly a helicopter around.

Keep it together.

"I brought you guys up here to go over a rescue in backcountry. Specifically, we're going to look at what was packed and how we would perform basic first aid when we have to hike in and carry out a patient."

"Couldn't you just fly in with the helicopter?" Jimmy asked, annoyed.

Candice's eyes narrowed. "This is in situations where you can't fly in."

"Then why did you fly here? Why didn't you hike in with us?" Jimmy snapped.

Stu, Kate and Nigel all looked at him in shock.

Candice crossed her arms and took a step toward him. "I would like to speak to you. Privately."

"Whatever you have to say can be said in front of everyone. I don't care."

What're you doing? Get a hold of yourself.

"No. I don't think so." Candice turned. "Nigel, can you start?"

Nigel nodded and motioned for Stu and Kate to follow him.

Jimmy sighed, annoyed with himself.

"What is wrong with you?" she asked tightly.

"Nothing."

"Nothing?" she echoed.

Jimmy scrubbed a hand over his face. "I know."

"You know?"

"I'm sorry. That was uncalled for."

"I won't tolerate anyone undermining me in front of the team. I am head of Mountain Rescue and I got here through hard work and firsthand experience. You may have experience in the armed forces, but this is *my* team. This is *my* mountain. Got it?"

"Yes. Got it. It won't happen again."

"See that it doesn't." She held his gaze for a bit longer. "Now, I would like to utilize your experience working in field hospitals by having you prepare a simple surgical kit for the field like we talked about yesterday. Do you think you can handle that?"

Jimmy nodded. "I can. Thanks, boss."

"Good," she said softly before walking away.

Jimmy ran his hand through his hair.

You're a boob, Jimmy Liu.

He wanted to tell her what was bothering him. He wanted to tell her about the PTSD, but then it would bring about talk of Logan and his death. He wanted to explain everything going on inside him, but he couldn't find the words.

He didn't want Candice to think less of him.

He didn't want Candice to see him as weak. It mattered to him what she thought of him, because he was a member of her team and he didn't want to be kept from work because of a stupid helicopter and the way it triggered him.

He wanted to have control of this. He would get control of this.

He couldn't be in the armed forces, but he could be doing what he loved again—saving lives in the place he never should've left.

Candice didn't know what had come over Jimmy.

He'd seemed fine last night when he dropped her off at her place after grocery shopping. Even though she had promised herself that she should avoid him, she had enjoyed the simple shopping excursion with him and his son.

Really enjoyed it. Which scared her.

She wasn't supposed to be enjoying herself with Jimmy.

He'd been back what, a day, and she was already falling into those old patterns. Old patterns she knew led to heartache and disappointment. Jimmy had left her. He'd told her he wanted more and then ended it. She had to remind herself of that. Jimmy was not the kind to settle down. He'd made that clear when he'd admitted that Marcus's mother was a one-night stand.

Still, she was concerned about his behavior. Something about the helicopter had triggered him.

Candice wasn't a fool. She knew it was most likely post-traumatic stress, which was concerning.

They used helicopters for a lot of rescues and she couldn't keep him aside every time they needed to do so. She wanted him on her team, in the thick of things. He was a competent and knowledgeable paramedic and she didn't want to waste his knowledge or his talent.

In fact, she was a bit jealous of his knowledge, if she was honest.

Why don't you go back to school?

She shook away the lingering thought. There was no way she could leave.

Jasper was her home and Mountain Rescue was her life.

As they were going through their equipment, she heard the distant sound of an engine. She turned to look and saw one of the Parks Canada vehicles coming toward them. The ATV pulled up and stopped.

"Lavoie, glad you're out here," Ranger Matt said as he parked his all-terrain vehicle.

"We're on a training session. What's up?" Candice asked.

Matt's lips pursed together under his bushy,

graying moustache. "There's a been a bear attack."

The rest of the team went quiet.

"I see," she said. Her stomach twisted in a knot. Bear attacks were never pretty. This would be grim.

"Do you need us? I have a paramedic with me."

"Yeah. We could use you both. Do you have your rifle with you?" Matt asked.

A shudder of fear ran down her spine. "I do."

"The bear is still on the loose. I'll help your team load up the helicopter. The trail has been shut down. You and your paramedic can come with me. We'll have to carry him out so we need to be careful."

Candice nodded and turned to her team. "Okay, let's get off the trail. I'll need a surgical kit. Jimmy, I want you to come with me—this will be a good learning experience—and, Nigel, I'll need my gun."

She tried not to pay attention to the worried expression on Jimmy's face as she grabbed her rifle and the gear she thought she might need.

She'd been a park ranger before she took her mountain-rescue training and she knew what to do when a wild animal went rogue, not that she relished it very much. She had no doubt the bear had attacked because it had had too many interactions with well meaning, but stupid, tourists, and had lost its fear of humans as a result.

She loaded her stuff in the back of the ATV and Jimmy joined her.

"I didn't know you knew how to use a rifle like that," he whispered stiffly. It was a Winchester Ranger. It was powerful enough to take down a bear at close range.

"Before I got into rescue I was a park ranger. I've had to put down a grizzly or two," she responded tightly. It was one of the worst parts of her job.

"That sounds awful."

"People don't know how to behave in bear country and they don't know how to give the animals space." She sighed. "I hope you're prepared for this. We're going to have to do as much damage control as we can and then carry the victim out. The helicopter can't land where the mauling took place."

"I've seen scary crap at the front lines. I'll be okay."

Candice didn't even want to begin to think about what Jimmy had seen overseas. She knew he'd been with Logan when he died. There were times she thought she wanted to know what had happened to her brother, but then there were times she realized it was better she didn't.

She remembered how her mother had fallen apart after losing Logan.

Candice had had to be strong for her dad through all of it. And for herself, when Chad had left. As a result, she'd never had the chance to really process Logan's death. Never had the chance to grieve, and now was not the time, either.

Candice had to remain strong and in control.

Like she had for the past ten years.

Ranger Matt came back. "We better go. Your team is ready to leave."

Candice nodded and she climbed in beside Matt while Jimmy got in the back with the equipment. Ranger Matt headed back down the trail the way he came, and though Jimmy winced as the helicopter started up, he visibly relaxed as they distanced themselves from the rotating blades.

The ride in the ATV was rough.

The farther they got down the trail, the thicker the brush got and she realized that the attack must have taken place close to the road. At least they'd be able to get an ambulance in to take the victim to the hospital.

She also realized that this attack had probably happened not long after her team had passed through here. She glanced back at Jimmy and could see that he was thinking the same thing, the closer they got. His lips were pursed and he looked serious.

Ranger Matt slowed down.

"The victim had been camping in an unauthorized spot and didn't check in with us to let us know he was planning to camp here. I suspect there wasn't proper food storage, but I'm not sure."

"So you don't know what provoked the attack?" Jimmy asked.

"We've been watching this bear as a matter of interest for some time—it's a problem bear—but there hadn't been an attack until now. Thankfully, he was scared off by a crowd of people—the ones who found the victim— and took off. Still, be on your guard. When a bear finds a food source, they come back. And this bear isn't one that's likely to give up free food."

A shiver ran down Candice's spine at the thought of the victim as food. It was her number-one fear living in the mountains.

Once they stopped, they all climbed out and Candice loaded her gear on her back and grabbed her rifle, following Ranger Matt's lead, with Jimmy between them.

As they drew closer, she saw the group of

hikers that had found the victim. They looked startled and upset, but uninjured, as the rangers took their statements.

"This way," Matt said grimly. "The patient was stable when I left to come find you, but it's bleak."

Candice swallowed the lump that had formed in her throat. They ducked under a low branch and she tried not to react to the scene of a destroyed campsite and the state of the attack victim's legs.

"Whoa," Jimmy said under his breath.

"This is bad," she whispered.

"I've seen worse," Jimmy said tightly.

They exchanged glances. Jimmy's brow was still furrowed, his lips a firm line, his jaw locked. Her stomach was doing flip-flops.

"I'm sure you have," she said, quietly.

"We can do this." Jimmy nodded. "Together."

She liked that firmness. That certainty. It grounded her.

"Yep."

She was glad Jimmy was back to his normal self. It gave her confidence that this would go well. They put on their gloves and made their way swiftly toward the patient. The man was only semiconscious, which was probably for the best. The rangers had managed to tie a tourniquet, which was stopping the man from bleeding to death.

"What's his name?" Jimmy asked over his shoulder.

"Ryan," a ranger said. Candice didn't see who the other ranger was, and she didn't care as she started pulling out her gear. She was trying not to let her thoughts overtake her at the sight of the man's mangled legs. She wasn't even sure that they could be saved.

The victim also had lacerations on his face and head from where the bear had grabbed him.

"You've seen worse?" Candice asked Jimmy nervously.

He nodded. "I have. We can only do our best to stabilize him and get him safely to the ambulance. The main thing right now is to stop him from bleeding out. The tourniquet was well done, but it won't hold for long."

"So what're you suggesting?" Candice asked. "We can't exactly sew his legs back on here."

"No, but I'm going to use hemostat. It'll stop him from bleeding out and then we can splint the legs and get him transported. First, I'm going to set up a central line."

Candice's eyes widened. "Here?"

He nodded. "Here."

"Just tell me what to do." She was eager to learn. She had always wanted to become a surgeon—that had been the plan before she'd had to leave school and return home.

All she could do was listen as he directed her. They inserted the central line, then Jimmy attached a bag of saline and Candice gave the victim oxygen, while Jimmy went to work making sure that the patient wouldn't bleed out on the mountain and that they would be able to move him.

Once Jimmy was sure everything was holding, they carefully stabilized the legs and then moved Ryan to the backboard.

"He's stable. We can transport him now," Jimmy called out.

Several of the rangers came and helped. They lifted up Ryan and carried him down the trail to the road, where the ambulance was waiting to take him to the hospital.

"You go," Candice said once they'd loaded him, taking a step back.

Jimmy nodded. "What about you?"

"I have to go with the rangers to look for the bear."

A brief moment of panic crossed Jimmy's face, but it disappeared. "You're going to go hunt a bear?"

"I'm a trained ranger. I know these woods.

You take care of Ryan." She smiled at him with reassurance. "I'll be fine. You did a good job, Liu."

Jimmy nodded, but he didn't look convinced that she would be fine and that annoyed her. She couldn't help but wonder if he still saw her as Logan's little sister.

That girl that used to be vulnerable.

That shy girl.

She wasn't that girl anymore.

Aren't you, though?

Tears stung her eyes, but she held back her emotions. She shut the ambulance door, banging on it to signal to the driver it was safe to go, and then watched it race away.

She was envious that Jimmy had medical knowledge she didn't have. Logan had once said that Jimmy would hold her back, but Jimmy had the skills she wanted. The family she wanted.

She was still that same person she'd always been.

Scared and lost.

CHAPTER SIX

WHAT'RE YOU DOING HERE?

Jimmy wasn't sure.

He'd arrived back at the station, after helping ensure Ryan was stabilized and in the hands of the doctors at the hospital, to find out that Candice hadn't returned from hunting that bear. It freaked him right out.

It was surreal seeing her with that rifle and knowing that she was putting herself in danger up on that mountain. He was worried about her.

When his shift was over, he went back to his parents' place to make sure that Marcus was okay and to spend some time with him, but he was on call for the night and Marcus was staying with his grandparents, so once he made sure Marcus was settled he went for a drive, taking his phone with him.

And the drive ended up at Candice's place.

Now, he was sitting on her porch, waiting for

her. At least the neighbors remembered who he was and no one was worried about a stranger sitting on Candice's porch, waiting in the twilight for her to return home.

Headlights turned the corner of the street and he sat up straighter. It was Candice's SUV. He stood up so that she could see him and wouldn't be frightened to find him there.

His heart was hammering. He was nervous and anxious and…he didn't know what else. Only when she parked her car and got out, looking no worse for wear, was he able to calm his anxiety and take a deep breath of relief.

She came up the drive and stopped, looking confused. "Jimmy?"

"Hey!" He waved.

"What're you doing here?"

"I wanted to make sure you were okay. You didn't come back to the station before my shift was over."

"Well, technically your shift is not over since you're on call tonight," she teased.

"I know, but still. You were tracking a bear. A bear! Did you end up finding it?"

"We tracked it, but didn't encounter it. We're hoping it went farther into the interior, but we'll have to put up warnings for the tourists and keep a lookout on the backcountry trails."

She sounded tired.

"I'm glad to see you're okay. That bear did a number on Ryan."

"How is the patient?" Candice asked, coming to sit beside him on the step.

"He'll live. I don't know about his legs, but the surgeons were very hopeful and they were impressed that I used my clamps so well. I explained to them where I learned it."

"I was impressed, too," she said softly. "And, truth be told, a bit envious."

"Envious?" he asked, confused.

"Yeah, you learned all these skills when you served. Skills I wanted to learn, but never got the chance."

"Why not?"

She cocked her head to one side. "You know why. I had my dad to take care of. There was never time."

"I can show you."

"You can?" she asked, perking up.

"Of course. If you want."

"I'd like that very much," she said.

An awkward silence fell between them as they sat there on her step, the sky fading from the purple hues of twilight to darkness.

"You hungry?" he asked.

"I am. I was going to go inside and make dinner."

"How about we go to the diner instead? I

saw that it was still there. I can't drink because I'm on call…but we could least have a hamburger or fries or something."

Great. You're starting to ramble.

"Sure. That sounds great."

"I'll drive, because I'm on call."

"I'm aware," she said dryly. "I'm the one who made the schedule."

He chuckled. "Oh, right. So it's you I have to thank for that. I forgot."

Candice laughed. The way she used to when they were together. When they were younger. When they didn't have a care in the world. It made him feel happy. It made him feel like a weight had been lifted off his shoulders. It made him feel free.

He missed that.

Jimmy opened the passenger door for her then climbed into the driver's seat. It wasn't a long drive to the small diner that sat at the edge of town, away from the tourist center and all the chain restaurants, and there were only a couple of cars in the parking lot.

Jimmy hadn't been sure it would still be here, so was glad when he'd come home to find it was still standing.

He parked the car and they made their way inside.

"Candice, good to see you!" The waitress,

Kelsey, said with a smile from behind the counter and then her eyes widened as her gaze landed on him. "My goodness! Is that Jimmy Liu?"

"Good to see you, Kelsey. It's been a while."

Kelsey grinned. "It has. I remember you all coming in here when you were kids!"

Jimmy chuckled. He'd missed that familiarity you only got in a small town.

"Sit anywhere you'd like," Kelsey said, before ducking into the kitchen.

He followed Candice to a booth in the corner.

Nothing had changed.

Still the same padded seats in the same blue and red vinyl. Same faux marble tabletops. It even smelled the same, like bacon grease and coffee. They looked out over the highway, the row of trees on the far side occasionally interrupted by a car or a truck passing through.

It was night and the campgrounds were closing down for the evening. The trails were already closed and the tourists were back in their lodgings or in town.

Jimmy was hoping for a quiet night, but usually when he'd hoped for a quiet night while serving overseas, he'd got the exact opposite.

"Marcus is with your mom?" Candice asked.

"He is. So he's safe, but I'm hoping that I

don't get a call tonight. I could use the sleep."
He crossed his fingers, holding them up for
her to see.

"Let's hope not. It's only your first week
here and it's been an eventful one, that's for
sure. Of course, it's always kind of busy when
we have a lot of tourists in town. In winter, ski
patrol picks up a lot of the slack, though there
are times we have avalanches and some other
issues, but summer seems to have a lot more
accidents and definitely more encounters with
wildlife."

Jimmy shuddered. "I don't remember a bear
attack like that when we were kids."

She smiled. "Well, we weren't working and
not every attack is reported. Besides, when we
were kids we didn't really care what was going
on around us."

"My mother would've made me aware of a
rogue bear," he said dryly. "She may have been
working all the time, but she was overprotec-
tive. Still is, just not with me now."

Candice laughed softly. "My grandmother
always said that grandkids were her pride and
joy. My mother always felt a bit snubbed."

"That could be it," Jimmy said.

"The trouble is that tourists are getting a bit
bolder with photos and selfies. It's a shame, really." There was a sadness in her voice. "Every

year, it just seems to get busier, and I sometimes long for the peace and quiet. If I didn't
love Jasper so much, I'd probably go farther
north."

Jimmy cocked his head to one side. "Would
you?"

"I've thought about it, but no, this is my
home. I'm happy here and I don't want to
leave."

He wanted to ask her why she wanted to
stay. She always had big plans. Her parents
were gone, so what was she staying here for?

She had said how much she wished she
could learn more and that she still wanted to be
a doctor. So what was keeping her in Jasper?

"Can I get you two something to drink?"
Kelsey asked, interrupting his thoughts.

"I'll have a coffee," Jimmy said and Kelsey
looked at him like he was crazy. "I'm on call
tonight."

She nodded and turned to Candice. "What
would you like, Candy?"

"The same. I'm also on call."

Kelsey nodded. "I'll be back with your coffee in a minute."

"I didn't know you were on call, too," Jimmy
said.

"You're still fairly new and you're still on
probation. When you're on call, so am I." She

smiled at him. "So how does it feel to be back home?"

"Strange," Jimmy said. "I never thought I'd come back here, but this is the best place for Marcus."

"How about you?" she asked softly.

"What do you mean?"

"Is this the best place for you?"

Jimmy nodded. "Yes. It is. I was a fool to leave."

He *was* a fool to leave, but both he and Logan had been so convinced that they could take on the world. They thought that they'd come back to Jasper as heroes.

Instead, Jimmy had returned defeated and Logan came back in a box.

His heart sank as he thought of that and he fought back the emotions running around inside him. He could hear the explosions, the gunfire, the screams in his mind.

Get a hold of it.

"You okay?" Candice asked.

"Of course," Jimmy said quickly, shaking the vision of Logan out of his mind. "Why wouldn't I be?"

"You just seemed to go somewhere else."

"I'm fine."

Liar.

"Here's your coffees. You ready to order?" Kelsey asked, interrupting them again.

"Banquet burger and fries," Jimmy said. He didn't even need to look at the menu to know that he wanted that large, greasy burger that had all the fixings. Just like he and Logan had always eaten, while Candice would have just a small cheeseburger and look at them in disgust as they shoved their fries in between the patty and the bun.

"I'll have the chicken burger, please, with a salad," Candice said.

"I'll get on this right away," Kelsey said as she turned to leave.

"Chicken burger and a salad?" Jimmy asked.

"What? I'm not feeling very hungry and don't want something heavy like your disgusting, greasy banquet burger." She shook her head. "You're getting older, Jimmy Liu— you might not be able to pack away the burger the same way."

"You mean by ramming the fries into it?" he teased.

"Yeah, exactly. You and Logan were so disgusting."

Jimmy laughed. "You chose to hung out with us."

"There was no one else to hang around with.

I liked hanging out with my big brother and…" She trailed off and pink tinged her cheeks.

"And me?" Jimmy asked, grinning.

"Sometimes," she said quietly, and there was the hint of something more in her dark brown eyes. Was it a flash of pain? He couldn't be sure…

"Thanks."

She chuckled, shaking off whatever heavy thoughts had rattled her. "It's the truth."

"Well, I'll try not to be too disgusting."

"Good. I appreciate it."

"I can't believe it's still here," he said wistfully. "I remember when we moved to Jasper. I was like…six, and we came here from Toronto. I was so exhausted and it was dark. This place was the only place open and I think Kelsey was working here then, too."

Candice smiled warmly at him. "She probably was. And, of course, this place is still here. This is an institution. Everyone comes here for Sunday lunch."

"Everyone except my parents. They were always working at the motel."

"I believe you came here a few times with us."

Jimmy smiled. "Your parents were always kind to me. My parents had a business to run so I was grateful that yours included me so much. They didn't have to."

There were unshed tears glistening in her eyes. "Yes. They liked you quite a bit."

Jimmy missed them, just like he missed Logan, and he felt so bad that he hadn't been there for any of them when they needed him.

"If I had of known..." He trailed off and shook his head. "About your dad."

"They understood. You were injured, too. Your parents were there. They came to every single funeral. Logan's, my mom's and my dad's. At least my parents are with Logan again."

"I have one banquet burger and fries and a chicken burger with a side salad," Kelsey said, cheerfully putting their plates down before them.

"This looks great, Kelsey. Exactly like I remember." Jimmy lifted the bun to add condiments.

Kelsey smiled. "You're welcome. Glad you're back, Jimmy."

She left them and Jimmy grabbed the ketchup.

"I'm so glad you're not jamming fries in there," Candice teased.

He cocked an eyebrow. "Who said I wasn't?"

In actual fact, he hadn't planned on doing

that, but now that Candice reminded him that he used to do it, he grabbed a handful of fries and started layering them on the top of his hamburger patty.

Candice was grimacing.

"Mmm..." he said, teasing her as he smooshed down the hamburger bun, squishing the fries and causing the ketchup and mustard to ooze out the side. He took a bite. "Yum."

She wrinkled her nose. "You're gross."

He winked and she laughed.

It felt good.

It felt right.

They finished their dinner and paid the bill before heading outside, into the dark. It was a peaceful night. There were stars in the sky, just like that night when they sat down by the river. She hoped it stayed this way. She was exhausted and could use a quiet night.

She hadn't planned for Jimmy's first night on call to follow a day of her hiking over the trails as they tracked a bear.

Even though they'd ridden in the all-terrain vehicle, there were some places the ATV couldn't get to and her legs were aching. And the bumpy trail had been hard on her posterior.

All she wanted was a hot shower and to go to sleep.

She hadn't been expecting to find Jimmy waiting for her on her porch, but she was glad he was.

It was confusing being around Jimmy. One minute they were laughing together, like no time had passed—almost like they could go back to the way things once were—and the next she was remembering the feeling of her heart being shattered when he walked away.

"I need to get home and change before I go back to the station," she said.

"I'll drive you home."

Say no. Say no.

Only, she couldn't. It made sense.

"Okay."

"I don't want to hang out at my parents' place. Marcus is not the best sleeper and it would be better for him to get used to the feeling of waking up at his grandma and grandpa's, because he'll need to stay with them when I'm on call."

"So where are you going to go?"

He shrugged. "My place or the station. Hadn't really thought which."

"Why don't you keep me company at the station for a while?"

She couldn't believe she was saying it, but she was lonely, too, and they were having a good time.

"Sure," he said. "If you don't mind."

"I don't. That way if we get a call, we can ride out together."

"Sounds like a plan."

They climbed into Jimmy's car and he drove them back to her place. When he parked in front of her house, she suddenly felt nervous and she didn't know why.

He'd been in the house before.

Nothing had really changed. She'd updated the decor a bit and added her own touches, but the furniture was the same.

It was still, in essence, her parents' place.

It was an easy way to keep them close and she really didn't have time to think about decorating, anyway. This was her home. This was where she felt safe—cozy and at peace.

"Come on in," Candice said, unlocking the door.

"Wow," Jimmy said in awe. "Nothing has changed that much."

"Why would it?"

"I don't know. I guess I thought you would put your spin on it or…"

"I don't have time for decorating. My dad's only been gone a year and it didn't feel right. This is home."

He smiled and nodded. "I'm glad you didn't change it, if I'm honest."

"Good."

Jimmy kicked off his shoes and jammed his hands in the front pockets of his jeans. He wandered into the front room, staring at the wood paneling that her father had painstakingly cut, stained and put up when her parents bought this house before she was born.

"Still the same," he said with satisfaction as he glanced out the bay window onto the dark street.

"Make yourself at home. I'll be back soon." She dashed up the steps to her bedroom. The only change she had made was taking over the main bedroom. Her father's cancer had prevented him from going up the stairs in the last few years of his life, so the dining room had been converted into his room.

She quickly changed and freshened up, grabbing her phone before she headed downstairs.

Jimmy wasn't in the living room. He had wandered to the back of the house, to the small den, where he and Logan had hung out a lot playing video games. The den had a sliding glass door that opened into a sunroom, and the sunroom had a door that led out onto a deck and into the backyard.

He was standing in the sunroom, in the dark, staring out at the forest. She could sense his sadness and she assumed he'd noticed the pictures of Logan. After Logan had died, her parents had turned the den into a bit of a shrine to him.

"You okay?" she asked quietly.

"Yeah," he said, barely glancing over his shoulder. "I wasn't… I wasn't expecting to see Logan's stuff."

"My parents wanted to display some of his things." She wandered into the room and gingerly touched Logan's picture, trying not to cry as she looked at his happy, smiling face.

Jimmy chuckled nervously under his breath. "I don't know why I didn't expect it. This is… This was Logan's home."

"You miss him?" she asked.

He nodded. "I do. He was my best friend."

"I know. I miss him, too."

Jimmy ran his hand through his hair and turned around. "I know. I wanted to be there…"

"We know you were injured and in hospital in Germany, Jimmy. We understood why you couldn't be here." What she didn't say was: *why didn't you come back after you recovered? Why did you stay away for so long?* But she couldn't make herself ask. "Want another coffee?"

He smiled and stepped out of the shadows. "That would be great."

She turned to head back to the kitchen and

Jimmy followed her. She flicked on the light and he took a seat at the kitchen table, in the same spot he always sat in when he'd come over for Sunday dinners, and for one brief second she thought she saw Logan sitting there beside him… Her parents, too. And for an instant, she was happy again.

It felt like it did all those years ago.

It's not the same.

Just because Jimmy was back in her life didn't mean that all that pain disappeared. A lot of water had passed under the bridge between the two of them and she had to remember that.

She shook her head and turned her back to Jimmy. "How do you like your coffee these days?"

"Black."

"Coming up."

"Your dad used to make this coffee that would cause our hair to stand on end. He'd make it when he and my dad would go out fishing and they'd take us. You know, the couple of times my dad would actually go. Grudgingly, but still. I almost wonder if your dad sort of forced him to come." Jimmy laughed. "My dad has hinted that your dad could persuade anyone to do anything."

Candice laughed. "Yes. He was a smooth talker."

"I loved those weekends," he said, reminiscing.

"I never got to go on those fishing trips," she said dryly.

"Well, it was a men's weekend."

She rolled her eyes but laughed. "Yeah, Dad liked those trips."

"So did my dad. We'd hike up to some remote lake, pitch our tents, fish…never catch anything, usually, but the coffee your dad gave us was like engine oil or something. You'd stay awake for days."

"I'm afraid my coffee is not like that." She pulled out a mug from the cupboard. "That recipe went with him to the grave."

"That's too bad, because one cup of that and being on call would be no problem…for a couple of days," he chuckled.

Candice poured him a cup and set it down in front of him. He blew away the steam and then she poured herself a cup and sat down in the chair across from him.

"So how far did you track the bear?" he asked.

"Pretty far off the trail. We're hoping it stays there, but I doubt it will. It's a problem bear and it's been getting bolder and bolder. I think it's only a matter of time before it comes back and we'll have to put it down."

"It's a shame."

"It is a shame." She sighed, trying not to think about it. "So you said Marcus is having a birthday soon?"

Jimmy nodded. "I did. He's turning two."

"Any ideas of what kind of party you want to have?" she asked, taking a sip of her coffee.

"Theme?" he asked, confused.

"Sure. Kids birthday parties usually have a theme."

"You know, my mom was asking about this, but I didn't pay any real attention to what she was going on about."

Candice chuckled. "What was she asking?"

"Whether he liked some goofy show with a pig or another show with dogs."

"Definitely go with the dogs. I've seen the pig show, it's annoying."

Jimmy laughed. "Yeah. Dogs it is."

"Good choice."

"You know, you should come to his party. It'll just be me, my parents and him, but he took a shine to you and I'd like you there."

Her heart skipped a beat. "You want me there?"

Jimmy smiled. "I do."

She didn't know what to say to that. She was

flattered. The little boy was cute and Jimmy was so tender with him. It had melted her heart to see him holding that boy so close, rubbing his back and tenderly kissing his head.

Jimmy was a good father and she was envious of his good luck.

And she wanted to go to Marcus's party… but then there was a part of her that said she shouldn't. That it would be a mistake to go, to get involved, to get too attached when her heart could be on the line. What if Jimmy met someone else? She couldn't be in their lives then. She didn't want to get hurt again.

But you want a family.

"Sure," she said, hoping he wouldn't notice the crack in her voice. "I would love to come. And if your mom needs any help or needs me to make a run into Hinton for supplies, I can do that."

"She'll hold you to that," Jimmy warned.

"I'm sure she will."

"It means a lot to me that you'd come to the party. You're important to me, Candice. One of the few people I know I can count on…" He paused and a look crossed his face that she couldn't quite read—a confusion, a hesitation, almost as though he was making up his mind about something.

Jimmy sighed. "Listen, I want to tell you

about my injuries and why I couldn't be there for the funerals. Something my parents don't even know. I owe it to you to tell you the truth."

"Okay," she said calmly, her heart racing.

"It took me a year to recover from my injuries."

She was shocked. "A year?"

"I broke both my legs and had shrapnel in my hip. It took some time to heal and walk properly again. I still have pain from time to time."

"So that's why it took you so long to come home and why you were discharged."

He nodded. "I wanted you to know. You're my boss, after all."

"Is that the only reason?"

His dark gaze pierced into her, mesmerizing her, holding her. "No, but I didn't want you to find out any other way."

She worried her bottom lip.

You have to tell him.

"There's something I want you to know then."

Her heart was racing faster. She got up from the table and started pacing, trying to calm her nerves. "That week we were together ten years ago…"

"I remember," he said hesitantly.

"After you left, I found out I was pregnant."

His eyes widened. She could tell he was in shock.

"What happened?" he asked quietly, clearly trying to process it all.

A tear slipped down her cheek and she brushed it away. "I miscarried. I'm sorry. I had no way to get ahold of you and I was hurt."

And you broke me.

Only she didn't say that. She didn't want to cry.

"Only my parents knew. I never told Logan."

Jimmy got up and put his arms around her. "Hey, I'm sorry."

She looked up at him, trembling, loving the way his arms around her made her feel so secure. So safe.

He touched her face. "I'm sorry I wasn't there, Candice."

She nodded. "Me, too."

Before she knew what had come over her, she stood on her tiptoes and kissed him. And it felt so right to kiss him again. Warmth spread through her and she melted in his arms all over again. The kiss deepened.

You need to end this.

Only, she couldn't. She didn't want to.

Her phone buzzed. She broke off the kiss and picked it up. There was an emergency text and her stomach sank when she read that the bear had come back. The message also contained the coordinates for a campground.

"We're up."

"What's wrong?" Jimmy asked, breathing deeply.

"The bear came back."

Her stomach was doing flip-flops on the drive to the campground. They had taken her SUV because it had everything they needed in the back.

Nigel had driven the ambulance out to meet them, even though when they answered the call, she was assured by the rangers that the campers had suffered only minor injuries and that the bear had been taken care of.

Still, it was Mountain Rescue's job to make sure that everyone was okay.

Thankfully, the campground was one of the main ones and they didn't have to hike in. But because it was a full campground, there were several people milling about even as the RCMP tried to keep the crowd under control.

Jimmy wasn't saying much. He had been smart and carried his first-aid kit in the back of his car, but she seriously doubted that they would need to do anything major tonight.

At least, that's what Constable Bruce had said when he'd called her.

Candice pulled up beside the ambulance as Nigel stepped out.

"Have you been waiting long?" Candice asked.

"Nah," Nigel said. "Just got here."

Nigel was trained to fly the helicopter and to drive the rig, but he wasn't a fully certified paramedic yet, which was why Jimmy was on call. She rotated between her paramedics and the rest of her team.

"They're over here," Nigel said. "Looks like a small laceration and a possible sprain. The bear did more damage to their tent."

"Still, I'll check them out and we'll probably have to take them to the hospital to get checked out if the bear caused the laceration," Jimmy said, slinging his pack over his shoulder. "They'll need antibiotics."

Nigel nodded and Candice followed them over to where a couple was sitting at a picnic table. Jimmy headed straight for the young woman because she was clearly bleeding.

"Hi, I'm Jimmy Liu and I'm the paramedic. What's your name?"

The woman smiled and Candice swore she was blushing a bit, but she wasn't surprised. Jimmy had that effect on women. "Traci."

"Traci, that's a nice name. Can you tell me

what happened?" he asked as he set down his pack and pulled out his head lamp and gloves.

"Sure," she said. "We were about to go to bed when this bear charged into our campground. It went straight for the tent and we ran. As I was running I hit my head on a branch and my husband, Derek, slipped and sprained his wrist."

"So the bear didn't cause your cut?" Jimmy asked, gingerly inspecting it.

"No." Her voice shook. "It was too busy tearing up our tent."

"You didn't have food in your tent, did you?" Candice asked.

Derek shook his head. "No. We're from Edmonton—we know what to do in bear country."

Candice nodded. "You got this, Jimmy?"

Jimmy nodded. "Yep. I'm going to clean it and use some dissolvable sutures. It's superficial. Then I'll check the wrist."

Candice nodded and made her way over to Ranger Matt, who was talking to Constable Bruce.

"So you got the bear?" Candice asked.

Ranger Matt nodded. "We did. I happened to be doing my patrol of the campground before the gates were shut and locked for the night just as the bear came through. The RCMP are talking to the other campers, as they're pretty shook up."

Candice could see a tarp and a large shape under it. She was sad seeing it there, but knew it had to be done to keep people safe.

"I'm going to check on my new paramedic. Thanks for keeping me updated," Candice said.

Matt nodded and wandered off with Constable Bruce. There was a truck now waiting to remove the bear.

Candice was just glad she didn't have to fill out paperwork that Matt would have to fill out. She made her way over to Jimmy as he was wrapping a tensor bandage around Derek's wrist.

"How's it going?" Candice asked.

"Good," Jimmy said. "Their injuries are minor and don't require a hospital visit, so Derek and Traci are going to go with the RCMP, who have arranged accommodations for them in town."

Candice nodded. "Good."

"Now, if the wrist is still throbbing tomorrow or, if you notice any kind of oozing or redness, please make your way to Jasper Urgent Care, okay?" Jimmy said.

"Sure thing. Thanks, Jimmy," said Derek as he put his good arm around his wife.

Jimmy cleaned up his stuff and then disposed of his gloves in the garbage in the back of the ambulance.

"I guess we should head back to the station and make our reports?" Jimmy asked.

"Yes."

As Candice turned to head back to her SUV, she heard something go "pop" and felt pain shoot up her leg. She crumpled to the ground, seeing a few stars before she passed out.

CHAPTER SEVEN

ALL SHE COULD FEEL was pain. In her ankle, her elbow and her face, but there was something else besides the pain—the awareness that she was floating in the air. As her eyes adjusted to the blurry darkness, she realized that not only had she lost a contact, which is why everything was blurry, but she was also being held by someone.

And that someone was Jimmy.

"Jimmy?" she asked.

"You fell," he said, his voice shaking a bit.

"How? It's flat here."

"You must've rolled your ankle and, in those boots, I'm worried you broke it. Your ankle has started to swell. We need to get you to the hospital."

She groaned. The side of her face and the back of her head were both hurting.

Of all the injuries she could've sustained in

her job, of course, she had to trip over her own feet and fall flat on her face in a campground.

She was humiliated.

And she was embarrassed that Jimmy was here to see it. At least she couldn't really see with one contact now missing.

Jimmy carried her into the back of the ambulance and set her down on the gurney. She winced, but kept her one eye shut.

"What's the matter?" Jimmy asked, his voice rising an octave, but she couldn't tell if he was panicked or worried or angry. He was just a blur—a navy uniform, flesh and a dark blob of hair on top. "Why are you keeping your eye closed like that?"

"I lost a contact and it's really hard to see. I also think the contact in my other eye is scratched, because it's pretty useless to see out of. You're a blur, and I'm getting a bit of double vision going on." She tiled her head and tried to make out his facial expression. It looked like he was frowning.

"Can you take out the other contact?"

"I will, but you need to get my spare glasses— they're in the glove compartment of my SUV."

"Cool, but right now I'd like to look at that ankle."

"I'll get them, boss. You said the glove box?"

Nigel asked. She hadn't even realized he was there, too.

"Yes. Thanks, Nigel," Candice said. She winced and sucked in a breath as Jimmy gently palpated her ankle through the boot.

"Yeah, it's swelling. We need to get this off." He undid the laces and gently removed the work boot, but it still hurt and she moaned a bit. "Sorry."

Next he took off her sock and even without good vision she could see the redness, the swelling of her ankle, and feel that it was hard to wiggle her toes without excruciating pain. She only hoped it wasn't broken and it was just a sprain.

"We're going to need to get this X-rayed to be safe," Jimmy said. "And your double vision is worrying me."

"What if it's just to do with the missing contact?" she asked, even though her head was throbbing and things were spinning.

"I seriously doubt that," he said dryly.

"Here are your glasses, boss," Nigel said, coming into the ambulance and handing the big, black frames to Jimmy.

"Thanks." Candice took out her one remaining damaged contact and tossed it into a garbage bag. Jimmy handed her glasses to her, but she had a hard time putting them on. "Dammit."

"Yeah," Jimmy chuckled gently. "It's just the contact."

He took the glasses from her and helped her slide them on gently. Everything kind of came into focus, but she still had a bit of double vision and the change in her focus made her stomach do a flip-flop.

"I'm going to be sick," she moaned.

Jimmy grabbed a kidney bowl just in time.

"Oh, God," she moaned, lying back and closing her eyes. It was better to close her eyes and she just wanted to sleep. She felt woozy.

"Hey," Jimmy said and she felt a cool cloth on her forehead. "Hey, don't sleep."

"I'm not," she murmured. "I feel awful. It hurts."

"I know it does," he said gently, touching her face. "I know."

Jimmy hated seeing her like this. When she rolled her ankle and fell, he'd dashed forward, trying to catch her, but he'd been too late and she went right into the gravel. He was furious with himself that he hadn't made it to her in time and was worried she had hit her head too hard. He was anxious about what it would mean if he was right.

Her ankle was turning an awful color and he was worried she'd broken it. From what he could tell, there was a small depression in the road and she'd stepped in it the wrong way and twisted too hard. It should never have happened. He should have been beside her, should have protected her. But once again he'd let her down.

He had to put that out of his mind. Right now he had to focus on taking care of Candice. He hadn't been there for her in the past, but he could be here now.

Guilt and panic drove him as he investigated her wounds. All he wanted to do was take care of her, to make the pain disappear.

"Nigel, could you get us to the hospital?" Jimmy asked as he carefully strapped Candice onto the gurney.

"Sure thing, Jimmy." Nigel climbed out of the back of the rig and shut the doors while Jimmy finished securing everything inside.

"Where are we going?" Candice murmured.

"To the hospital," he said calmly. The last thing he wanted to do was agitate her.

"Right."

"Do you have an emergency contact I could call?" he asked.

"Nope," she said. "They're all gone."

His heart sank a bit. "You don't have anyone? Not an uncle or cousin or anything?"

"Nope. No one left," she murmured. "I have

a couple of friends in my phone. Not a lot of time to make friends when you're the boss, though."

"You have me," he whispered, but she didn't respond. He didn't expect her to, but it was true. Sure, he'd been gone for a long time, but he was here now and he wasn't going to leave her.

Nigel turned on the lights, but he didn't put the siren on. They didn't have a dire need to get to the hospital, as Candice had Jimmy looking after her.

Jimmy sat watching Candice carefully as she drifted in and out of consciousness and it was freaking him out a bit.

He leaned over the gurney and touched her gently. He smiled as he watched her.

He'd always thought she was beautiful. Before Logan had died, he'd asked Jimmy for one thing—to take care of Candice—and that was what he would do right now.

"I know I said keep away from her," Logan had whispered all those years ago, when they'd been trapped, *"but you have to promise me you'll look out for her. Promise me. I know she cares for you."* He was repeating himself again.

"You can take of Candy yourself when you get home," he said frantically.

Logan shook his head and Jimmy saw the light fading from his best friend's eyes, the chaos of war going silent as he had watched his best friend slip away.

"Tell her... Tell her I love her and take care of her."

"I will, Logan. But hang on. Just hang on."

"I can't. I can't..." his friend had repeated...

"I'm here," he whispered again now, his voice catching as he touched her face gently. "I'm here and I'm not going anywhere."

She opened her eyes and sort of smiled at him. "You're where?"

He chuckled. "Here."

"Good," she sighed, drifting off again.

"Hey, you need to wake up."

She groaned. "If I wake up I'll be sick."

"I'll catch it," he teased.

She laughed a bit. "Gross."

Jimmy chuckled softly to himself.

The ambulance pulled into the bay, so Jimmy got up and grabbed everything as Nigel opened the back doors.

Together, they lifted the gurney out of the ambulance into the hospital.

Thankfully, it wasn't busy, and Candice was immediately taken into an emergency-room pod, where Jimmy helped move her off the gurney into a bed.

"You going to stay?" Nigel asked.

"Yeah. We can call a cab to come get us when she's discharged. You okay to get back to the station?"

Nigel nodded. "No worries. The next shift will start soon. I'm almost off duty, but if you're okay to stay…?"

"I'm okay to stay. She doesn't have anyone else."

Nigel nodded. "I'll see you later then."

"Thanks, Nigel."

Nigel left and Jimmy took a seat in the chair beside the bed as they waited for Candice to be triaged and assessed.

"Where is my SUV?" Candice moaned.

"At the campground. It's fine. We can get it tomorrow. Ranger Matt knows what's going on."

Candice sat up, wincing and touching her head. "What is going on? Where am I?"

"In the emergency room. You rolled your ankle and I think you have a concussion. We need to get it checked out."

She glared at him in disbelief, her black glasses sliding down the bridge of her nose. "As if."

"Really." He tried not to laugh at her bizarre behavior, which was a classic sign of a concussion. It would take time for her brain to heal if that was the case, and her being alone worried him. She would have to be monitored.

"I'm Dr. Zwart—what seems to be the problem?" Dr. Zwart looked up from his clipboard. "Oh, Lavoie, I didn't know it was you!"

"Hi," Candice said brightly, before lying back down, obviously dizzy again.

"I'm Jimmy Liu. I'm a paramedic with Mountain Rescue."

"Pleasure—can you tell me what happened?" Dr. Zwart was already staring at the ankle, which was bruising.

"We responded to a call about a bear and I tended to a minor laceration and a sprained wrist. Candice went to speak to the rangers, stepped in a hollow, rolled her ankle and face-planted onto the gravel road. She's had some double vision, nausea, dizziness and peculiar behavior."

"So she needs to be checked for a concussion," Dr. Zwart stated. "Tell me about the ankle."

"She can't put weight on it and it started swelling fast. I removed the boot and elevated it the best I could. I did do a palpation, but it's so swollen I'm not sure if the bone might be broken."

Dr. Zwart nodded. "We'll do an X-ray. You

can head back to your rig, Liu. We've got it from here."

"With all due respect, Candice doesn't have anyone else. She's not only my boss, but a family friend. We grew up together and I would like to stay."

Dr. Zwart nodded and tilted Candice's head to look at the scrape. "Sounds good. I'll order some tests and I'll have the nurse clean up the facial laceration, which appears to be a superficial scrape, but still, as it was the gravel road in the campground we better get it checked out."

"Thanks, Dr. Zwart. Is there a phone nearby?"

"You can use the one there by the nursing station. Just dial nine to get an outside line."

"Thanks, Doc." Jimmy got up and headed to the nursing station. Picking up the phone, he dialed home to speak to his mother.

"Hey, Mom," he said.

"Jimmy? Is everything okay?" his mom asked, panic in her voice. "It's almost midnight."

"I'm okay, but Candice is in the hospital. She might have a concussion and a fracture. She doesn't have anyone else, so I've got to stay with her to monitor her for the next twenty-four hours if it's a concussion. Unless the concussion is bad, they won't keep her here."

"I understand," his mom said gently. "She's a good girl. Don't you worry about Marcus. He'll be fine with his *nǎinai*."

"Thanks, Mom. I appreciate it." He hung up the phone and headed back to the curtained-off bed, where a nurse was cleaning Candice's face.

"You're Candice's emergency contact?" the nurse asked.

"I am. I'm Jimmy Liu."

"Good. She's going to have to take off her uniform to have the X-ray because there's metal in it. Could you step out while I get a gown on her?"

"Sure."

"Good." The nurse finished cleaning up Candice and closed the curtain, opening it a few moments later. "We're going to take her to get an X-ray. You can wait here." The nurse lifted the side bar of the bed, preparing it for the journey down the hall.

"Jimmy, are you coming?" Candice asked.

"No. I'll stay here," he said. "I'll be waiting for you."

"Okay." She frowned.

Jimmy stepped out of the way as they rolled the bed out of the curtained room and off to X-ray.

He wished he was going with her. It pained him to let her out of his sight.

He was worried about her, worried he had let her down again, worried he'd let down Logan by not honoring his promise to look out for her.

And he was also worried about himself.

He still wanted Candice after all this time and that was a worrisome prospect indeed. She was single and free, yes, but she still had dreams to fulfill, dreams Jimmy still worried he would hold her back from.

He promised Logan he'd take care of Candice and he would do that by making sure she fulfilled her dream. Which meant setting aside his feelings for her.

The hospital called Jimmy a cab once all the tests on Candice were completed. He managed to help her get dressed, but the giddiness was wearing off and it was quickly replaced with exhaustion. He was feeling it, too.

He was relieved when Dr. Zwart announced the ankle was just a bad sprain and should be right as rain in a couple of weeks, and that the concussion was a grade one and she would only have to be monitored for forty-eight hours before her follow-up appointment.

It could've been a lot worse.

And he was glad it hadn't been.

He paid the cab driver, leaving Candice in the car while he opened the front door of her house, and then picked her up out of the taxi and carried her up the porch and into her house.

He shut the door with the heel of his boot and the slam roused her.

"Where are we?" she said weakly.

"You're home." He didn't know where to put her, and then he saw a bedroom in what used to be the dining room and remembered her saying that her father had used that room. "I'm going to put you on the couch and then I'm going to make up your dad's bed, okay?"

"Okay."

He set her down gently and then made his way upstairs. The linen closet was still in the same place and he pulled out a spare set of sheets, then headed into her room to grab her pillows, but her old room was empty. It was only then he remembered she said that she'd moved into the master bedroom.

While the rest of the house was still her parents' home, this room was hers. And it suited her. It was modern and clean, with soft colors, and looked comfortable and calming.

When he picked up her pillows, he could smell that vaguely vanilla scent that was distinctly hers.

Focus, Jimmy.

He piled up her quilt and pillows on the sheets he'd grabbed, then found an oversized nightshirt and grabbed some of her toiletries. Everything was precariously perched, but he managed to get downstairs without dropping anything.

He set everything on the spare bed and made quick work getting the room prepared for her. Once it was ready, he went back into the living room and picked her up.

"Can I sleep now?" she asked.

"Soon. Let's get this uniform off," he whispered.

"Okay." Then she giggled. "But usually men buy me a drink before that."

Good lord.

"Would you just cooperate?" he asked firmly.

Candice stuck out her bottom lip. "Okay."

It's not like she's getting totally naked. Just out of her uniform.

That's what he had to keep reminding himself as he helped Candice out of her shirt. He kept his eyes averted, but her silky hair brushed his cheeks. Her hair still smelled like vanilla, but just faintly.

Exactly the way he remembered.

Focus.

Now came the tricky part. He had to get her out of her trousers.

"Do you think you can stand?"

"No, but I can try."

"Put your arms around my neck." He reached down to undo her belt.

"Okay."

His blood heated as his hands skimmed her soft skin.

She's concussed. Get a hold of yourself.

He was inwardly cursing every deity of bad luck he could think of for putting him in this situation. A few hours ago, they had been kissing in her kitchen, and now Candice was swaying back and forth and laughing.

"What's so funny?" he asked, frustrated.

"Jimmy Liu is undoing my pants!"

He rolled his eyes, glad no one else was around to hear this.

"Jimmy Liu's hand is on my butt!"

"My hand is not on your butt. Not right now, anyway. Step out of your trousers slowly."

She stepped out, one leg at a time and he caught sight of the tattoo. The sexiest tattoo of a feather he'd ever seen. Well, it wasn't so much the tattoo, but the placing of it on her inner thigh and the fact it was Candice.

He remembered how much he liked to kiss that tattoo.

Focus.

He helped her put on her nightshirt and then climb into bed, gingerly lifting her swollen ankle up onto a pillow. She was watching him petulantly and he couldn't help but smile at her.

"Thanks," she said.

"You're welcome, but you owe me a drink or something," he muttered, folding her uniform.

"I'll never remember that."

"I know."

"Sorry."

"What?" he asked.

"I need the bathroom."

He rolled his eyes. "Okay. Let's get up. You're worse than Marcus, you know."

He helped her to the bathroom and waited outside while she cleaned herself up. When she opened the door, he carried her to bed. He settled her against the pillow and arranged the pillow at her feet to elevate her leg, before doing a final tuck of her quilt.

"There. You're snug as a bug in a rug."

She smiled dreamily at him. "I never understood that."

"What?" he asked.

"The bug in a rug."

He chuckled. "Me, either."

"Are you going to leave?"

"No," he said. He wasn't going to leave

her—not tonight. And there was a part of him that didn't ever want to leave her. "I'll sleep on the couch."

"Can you stay for a bit longer?" she asked, patting a spot next to her on the bed.

"Okay." He sat down gingerly.

"Thank you for being with me tonight."

"You're welcome."

"You know how I feel about you," she said.

His pulse quickened. "Pardon?"

"I loved you and you left. It hurt, but it's okay that you don't feel that way about me."

Jimmy could tell that she was a bit out of it. That this was the concussion talking and Candice probably wouldn't remember any of this in the morning.

"I cared for you," he said gently.

"You did?"

He nodded. "Logan didn't want me to hold you back."

"Hold me back?" she asked, confused.

"From going away to medical school, but I've always cared for you." He reached down and touched her face, brushing his knuckles over her soft, silky cheek.

Candice leaned forward and touched his face, too. "I wanted you to be my first. I'm glad you were."

And before he could stop her, she kissed

him, gently, and then it deepened into a longing, lingering kiss. He cupped her face, not wanting the kiss to end, reveling in the feeling of her soft, full lips against his.

The kiss broke and he let Candice lie back down, her eyes closed as she drifted off into sleep.

His blood sang with unrequited longing. He wished that their kitchen kiss could have continued and that she might remember this conversation.

He certainly wouldn't forget.

CHAPTER EIGHT

CANDICE WOKE WITH a start. She'd been having a lovely dream, where she was kissing Jimmy and could still feel his lips against hers. But the sensation faded as her aches and pains claimed her attention—her pounding head, her throbbing ankle.

As her eyes adjusted to the light, she realized she was in her father's old bedroom and she was in one of her pyjama shirts, but still wearing her bra and underwear.

What the heck happened?

She tried to roll over and get up, but couldn't.

Candice managed to grab her glasses, which were sitting on a side table, and as she put them on the world came into greater focus. As she looked around the room, she noticed that Jimmy was slumped over and snoozing in her father's old recliner by the window. Her heart skipped a beat and she touched her lips. Had it been a dream or had it really happened?

"Jimmy?" she whispered.

He woke with a start. "Hey, you okay? You need something?"

"Answers," she said and cleared her throat. "And maybe some water."

"Well, you're due for some acetaminophen. Hold on, I'll be back." He got up and quickly left the room, returning a few moments later with medication and a big glass of water. "Take two. Dr. Zwart said you have a grade-one concussion and you're going to need a bit of time to heal."

Well, that explained the hazy memories and the bizarre dreams. Since he wasn't mentioning their kiss, it must've been a dream, but there was a part of her that suspected it hadn't been. That it had really happened and even though she would be mortified if that was the case, she was hoping it had.

"A concussion? I can't take time off for a concussion. I'm supposed to do the backcountry loop on the weekend."

"Yeah, even if you didn't have a concussion, your ankle is kind of really sprained. I doubt you're doing a hike on the weekend."

Candice groaned as she got a closer look at her purple-and-red swollen ankle.

"What the heck happened?" she asked.

Jimmy sat down on the edge of her bed.

"You stepped into a hollow the wrong way, rolled your ankle and face-planted onto the road in the campground."

Candice groaned. "Are you serious?"

"Yes, and we've had this conversation before."

She winced and vaguely remembered bits and pieces of last night, but a lot of it was a blur. "Where's my car?"

"Ranger Matt drove it to the RCMP office. It's just down the street, so I'll grab it later."

"You stayed here all night?" she asked.

He nodded. "I did."

Heat bloomed in her cheeks as she looked at her state of undress. "You—you…undressed me?"

"Yes." There was a twinkle in his eyes. "You were a bit, uh, sick…on your uniform."

She groaned and lied down again. "I'm so sorry."

"You weren't sick on me," he teased.

"I'm so embarrassed."

"Don't be."

The thought of him undressing her brought a blush to her cheeks. Her body thrummed and she wished she could remember more of it. She had no doubt he was a gentleman about it, and she was still a bit embarrassed, but there was another part of her that was slightly thrilled at the idea of Jimmy undressing her. His hands on her again.

She only wished she remembered it. And that she could have been a willing participant, undressing him, too. The thought of undressing him slowly, running her hands over his body, exploring that tattoo and his muscles, made her heart beat faster, her blood heat.

Don't think about him like that. You don't want to get hurt again and he's not in to you.

"What about Marcus?" she asked, changing the subject and getting her mind off of Jimmy naked with her, his hands on her.

"I told my mom what happened and she has Marcus. He's fine. You need someone to stay with you for the next couple of days and I can do that."

"Why?" she asked.

"Is there anyone else?" he asked quietly. "My place is small. It's better for you to stay put here."

"What about Marcus?"

"I can bring him by, if that's okay? And besides, my mother would love to clean my place thoroughly and finish my unpacking so she can root out secrets." He was teasing and winked at her.

She smiled. "Yes. I'd like it if you'd bring Marcus by."

And that brought her right back to reality. No, there was no one else in her life. She was alone and it was something she'd never really allowed herself to think about, instead keeping herself busy with work.

Her parents had been only children. She didn't have any cousins or aunts or uncles or anyone. Logan and her parents had been her family and they were gone. It scared her to think of being vulnerable and alone, with someone she didn't know making decisions for her.

"Thank you for taking care of me," she said soberly, shaken to her very core by the simple realization that she had no one.

It hurt.

"Hey," Jimmy said, softly inching closer to her. "It's okay."

She brushed away a tear. "Sorry."

"You've been through a lot. You have a grade one concussion and a bad sprain. Yeah, it's not an ideal time to take time off of work, especially with an annoying new employee, but I'm here for you, okay?"

She nodded, sniffling. "Thanks, Jimmy. I really appreciate it."

"No problem. Now, sit back and relax." He stood up and placed a set of crutches close to her bed. "Since you have a concussion, I'm afraid you can't watch television or read or look at your phone, so… I thought you might like to listen to a podcast or an audio book or something?"

"No thanks," she said, her head pounding. "I think I'm going to try and make it to the bathroom and then come back and rest."

"Okay. I'm going to run up the street and get your SUV. I'll be gone twenty minutes. You going to be okay?"

She nodded. "I'll be fine. Go."

"Okay." Jimmy slipped out of the dining room and left the house. She craned her neck to see him jog down her sloped driveway in the direction of the RCMP station.

Candice sighed and leaned back against the pillows.

She tried not to cry, but it was hard not to. There were so many emotions playing with her. She blamed her head injury on her inability to keep it under control and then she laughed as she thought that only she could manage to get a concussion rolling her ankle and doing a face-plant on a gravel road.

She sat up and grabbed the crutches. It took a couple of tries to get herself up, but once she was up she moved easily to her father's bathroom.

After cleaning herself up and finding a

change of clothes neatly laid out for her, she managed to make her way out of the dining room and to the kitchen, just as Jimmy pulled up in her driveway.

He came bounding up the steps and back into the house.

"Where are you going?" he asked when he saw her creeping down the hall.

"I'm hungry."

His eyes widened and he smiled. "Well, that's a good sign."

"Yeah, the pain in my head is dissipating. So if I take it easy the next few days I should be okay."

"You're still not cleared to drive or anything. Dr. Zwart wants you to follow up with him in forty-eight hours."

She nodded. "I understand."

He followed her into the kitchen and made her sit at the table. "What would you like?"

"Just some toast. I better take it easy."

Jimmy nodded. "Toast, it is."

He found her half loaf of bread and popped two slices into the toaster.

"What about Marcus's party?"

"Well, I do have to relieve my mom later, but she promised to come sit with you. She wants to take you up with your offer to help with the party, but no reading or writing. Nothing that requires too much thinking power."

Candice chuckled. "I'm not the best party planner, but I'd love to help and to keep busy."

"You picked the right theme. Dog over pig."

"That's pretty easy. I told you, that pig is annoying."

He grinned at her and her heart skipped a beat. "You know, I can't believe you're still wearing the same glasses."

"They're in fashion again, but they're not the same glasses," she said. "They're upgraded and not out of the discount bin, where my dad liked to shop."

Jimmy chuckled. "Well, they do suit you. I always liked those type of frames. They scream 'sexy librarian.'"

Heat bloomed in her cheeks and all she could think about was the kiss she'd dreamed about. But was it just a dream?

"Jimmy, about yesterday… Did we…? Did I do anything out of the ordinary once we got back from the hospital?"

He turned his back to her as the toast popped up. "What do you mean?"

There was an odd tone to his voice and she knew that something had happened. Maybe her dream wasn't a dream. Maybe they had actually kissed.

Oh. No.

"I mean, you did suggest I buy you a drink when I was trying to get your pyjamas on," he teased.

"I mean, did we kiss?"

"Before or after the concussion?"

She moaned. "I know we did before, but I'm not sure about after."

He chuckled. "It's okay. Like I said, you were a bit out of it."

"Still."

She was embarrassed.

She didn't want to get hurt by him again and she was his boss—kissing him once was unprofessional, but twice? Inexcusable.

He set down the toast in front of her and then got her some butter. "There you go."

"Are you going to sit around here all day watching me like a hawk?" she asked.

"Pretty much."

"I appreciate it, but I think I can manage."

He shook his head. "Don't be stubborn. Dr. Zwart said that you needed to be watched closely for the next forty-eight hours, so that's what I'm going to do. I have to leave you for a bit today to be with Marcus, but like I told you, my mom will come sit with you. Thankfully she's bringing me a change of clothes. I'm about ready to ditch this uniform."

"I wish I had some clothing to offer you, but I doubt you'd fit in anything of mine."

"Purple isn't really my color, but thanks," he said, pouring himself a cup of coffee he'd brewed earlier.

"I'm sorry that I'm taking you away from Marcus." She meant it. A kid needed his dad around.

"It's okay. He's young and you need help. It's the least I can do. You're my friend and Logan was my friend." He frowned and then poked at his coffee cup, pushing it slightly. The mood shifted and she could feel the sadness permeating the air.

She felt it, too, whenever she thought of Logan.

Candice set down her toast, which now tasted like sawdust in her mouth. Her head started to throb.

"I think I'm going to lie down again. My head is hurting." She stood up and grabbed her crutches, making her way out of the kitchen. "Thank you for the toast."

"No problem. If you need anything else, let me know."

"I will," Candice called over her shoulder as she hobbled down the hall and made her way back to her father's old room. She really needed to put some space between them.

* * *

After Candice went back to bed, Jimmy stepped out onto the deck and made his way down to the forest. He could hear the water from the edge of the property and he made his way through the trees to the small clearing where he and Logan used to sit down by the spring's edge.

The two stumps they had once sat on were still there, though a bit overgrown now with long grass and moss.

He sat down on his stump and stared out over the water.

"I know you said you didn't want me to start anything with her, but it's not easy, Logan. She's a great person." Jimmy scrubbed his hand over his face, annoyed that he was talking to himself.

Things would have turned out so differently if he had known that Candice was pregnant before he left. He would've stayed. Would have been there for her, experienced all the excitement at the prospect of a baby, and held her in his arms when that dream was shattered.

Instead, he'd been thousands of miles away and had had no idea any of it was happening. But maybe that was for the best. If he'd stayed, there was always the chance that Logan would have been proven right—that Jimmy would have held back Candice and she would have ended up resenting him.

Jimmy took a deep breath and got up from the stump. He wandered back to Candice's home and made his way back inside. He went to check on her, but she wasn't sleeping, like he thought she might be.

Instead, she'd gotten dressed with the clothes he'd laid out for her and she was sitting on the couch with another cup of coffee.

"There you are," she said when he came back in. "Where were you?"

"I thought you were sleeping so I went for a walk in the woods. Sat on the stump chairs that Logan and I used to chill at."

"I'm glad you found them. Dad always refused to get rid of them."

"I'm glad he didn't. How did you get another cup of coffee?" he asked, taking a seat on the coffee table by the couch.

"I made it?" she said, confused.

"You're supposed to be resting."

"I'm not an invalid, Jimmy. You can't stay here forever. I can manage on my own—I have to manage on my own."

"I don't plan on staying here forever," he snapped. "But you need to rest and someone is supposed to stay with you for forty-eight hours."

"You have your son. You can go. I can manage," she said stiffly.

Of course she didn't need him. She'd been on her own for so long.

"You need me now," he responded. "You needed me yesterday, when you hurt yourself and you were out of sorts. You told me that you needed me."

Her eyes widened and the blush rose in her cheeks as she sat up. "What?"

Jimmy kneeled in front of her. "I'm happy to be here, Candy. I made a promise to Logan. When he died, he asked me to take care of you."

Tears filled her eyes and one slipped down her cheek. "What? He said what?"

He brushed away the tear. "I'm here for you."

Candice trembled under his touch and all he could think about was kissing her again. His pulse was thundering between his ears and he recalled the way she had kissed him last night. She didn't remember that and he wanted her to remember it.

He wanted her to remember their kiss.

He cupped her face and leaned in.

"Jimmy? Candice?"

Jimmy jumped back and Candice wiped the

tears from her eyes as Jimmy's mother walked in, carrying a bag of groceries.

"Mom, what're you doing here?" Jimmy asked.

"It's one o'clock, you told me to come by." His mother's eyes flickered between him and Candice and he swore he saw a secret little smile. "I brought Candice some lunch. Some of my broth, too."

"Thank you, Mrs. Liu," Candice said, her voice shaking. "I appreciate it."

"Call me Liena," his mother said, smiling warmly. "I'll just put these into the kitchen?"

"That would be great, Liena," Candice said.

"I'll be back," Jimmy said. He followed his mother into the kitchen. "Is Marcus with Dad?"

"Yes," Liena said, puttering around Candice's kitchen. "Marcus loves being with his *yéye*, and Yéye loves being with him, but Marcus is missing you. You go spend some time with your son and I'll take care of Candice."

As much as Jimmy wanted to stay with Candice, he wanted to check on Marcus. Though he was a bit terrified at the prospect of his mother watching Candice, someone had to stay with her and his mother was the only person who had offered.

His mother had always had a soft spot for Logan and Candice Warner.

And it would also be nice to change out of his uniform and shower.

"Okay. I'll be back by this evening," Jimmy said.

His mother waved. "Go. Don't worry about it. I'll take care of her like she's my own daughter."

Jimmy paused as his mother began to hum and put things away. If he didn't know any better, he would assume that his mother was plotting something. Sometimes he could never be sure what Liena Liu was thinking, and he knew his mother was a persistent force to be reckoned with on the best of days.

Jimmy left the kitchen to find Candice sitting upright on the couch.

"How's the ankle?" he asked.

"It doesn't feel as swollen. The elevating is working."

"Well, let me check before I go." He kneeled down in front of her and unwrapped the tensor bandage. The swelling had definitely gone done, which was good.

"I was going to attempt a shower," Candice said. "Do you think you can leave the bandage off for a bit?"

"Okay, but I'll wrap it tonight before you go to bed."

"You're coming back?" Candice asked.

"I know you can manage on your own or whatever," he teased, trying to make light of the awkward situation from before. "I'm just following Dr. Zwart's advice. I'll just be here a couple of nights and then you'll be on your own."

Candice smiled. "Okay. Fine."

"Glad you're accepting your fate," he quipped. "Not like you had much of a choice, though."

"Go spend time with your son," she said. "I'll see you later."

Jimmy stood. "Okay. By the way, my mom is stocking your kitchen. I'm sorry."

She smiled. "It's fine. It'll be nice to spend time with her."

"Try to sleep or she'll talk your ear off." He left Candice sitting on the couch and his mother in the kitchen. His stomach flip-flopped with anxiety, but he had no choice.

He needed a shower and he needed some space from Candice before he tried something utterly foolish, like kissing her again.

CHAPTER NINE

As MUCH AS she fought Jimmy coming to take care of her at first, she was glad that he had and grateful to Mrs. Liu for staying with her while Jimmy was spent time with his son. She did her best to help Liena with planning Marcus's birthday party, but she kept dozing off. She only hoped she'd be well enough to attend.

Jimmy came back that evening and she convinced him to spend the night sleeping upstairs in her room instead of cramped on the couch or in the chair by her bed again.

The next day Marcus came over and she got to enjoy watching the little toddler run all over her backyard. Jimmy's rental didn't have much of a yard to play in, so Marcus was in his element, running and stretching his little legs, and Candice got the pleasure of watching Jimmy interact with his son.

She only wished she could join them.

After forty-eight hours, she was able to get

around okay, and when she had the checkup with Dr. Zwart, he cleared her to drive and do some other stuff, but to do those things slowly. He wasn't ready to clear her for work, though, and told her she couldn't go back for a week.

Jimmy, on the other hand, had to return to work, so she made sure that Stu and Nigel would take him under their wings. Jimmy was a capable paramedic, but he was still a new member to Mountain Rescue. Stu, her second in command, was a competent trainer, but she'd feel so much better when she got back to work and could see Jimmy's progress for herself.

When Jimmy was done his shift for the night, he would come by and check on her, and she quickly got used to how nice it felt to have someone look in on her. To have someone that cared.

She just didn't want to get used to relying on that particular human connection, because if Jimmy found someone else, started dating someone else, he wouldn't make time for his late best friend's little sister.

Who said he's going to date anyone else?

She ignored that little thought in her head.

A man like Jimmy Liu wouldn't stay single for long. She'd seen how the other girls in their school had reacted around him. He was handsome, charming and smart. And he'd only gotten more appealing with age—being a first responder meant that he was in good shape, and he was a good father. Anyone who wasn't obtuse could see the way he doted on his son.

He was a catch.

Why can't he be your catch?

That, she didn't know. Other than she was afraid of the toll that losing him would take on heart again.

"Hey!" Jimmy said, coming into her house after his shift. He paused when he saw her sitting on her steps. "What's up? You look really angry."

"I'm going stir-crazy," Candice muttered. "My foot is still a bit too swollen to get on my sneaker, but I don't like driving in my flip-flops to Hinton."

"Why are you going to Hinton?" Jimmy asked.

"I need to go into a larger town for supplies."

"Should you be doing that?"

"Dr. Zwart said I could, but I wasn't going to go until I got my foot to fit my sneaker, which it doesn't." She tossed away the sneaker. "I wanted to get Marcus a present and there's a better selection of stuff in Hinton."

"Well, why don't I drive you?"

"You just came off an overnight shift."

He shrugged. "I'm not tired and, anyway, my mom tasked me with going into town to get some stuff for the party. We can pick up Marcus and take him out to lunch, or to a bigger park. And best of all, you can wear your flip-flops!"

Say no.

Only, she was going stir-crazy and she liked spending time with Jimmy and Marcus. She'd been off work for a week and she'd seen them frequently. She was getting used to having them around, glad they lived down the street and she saw them often.

"Okay." She smiled. "Let me grab my purse and we can go."

"Sounds good. I'll meet you at the car."

She grabbed her things and locked up her place.

Jimmy was waiting at the bottom of the porch steps and he helped her down, as she was still limping a bit.

She wasn't used to hanging around at home.

She was used to working, or flying in the helicopter, or being up on the mountain doing a rescue, or doing her rounds with the rangers. It kept her busy. It kept her mind off everything else and spending the last few days just sitting there, unable to do anything, her mind had bombarded her with a lot of stuff she thought she'd locked firmly away.

So even though this was putting her heart on the line, she was thankful for the errand and the excuse to go out. Jimmy took her hand and they ambled to his car.

"You're walking a lot better."

"I've been working hard on some stretching and physio. I plan to be going back up my mountains by next week."

"You're ambitious."

"I have a backcountry loop to walk. I had to switch. I was supposed to be doing that last weekend when I got hurt."

"I know. And Stu still wants me to go with you."

"We can't have two paramedics on the loop. We always need a couple in Jasper. That's why he doesn't want you to go with him."

"And Stu doesn't want to take a 'greenhorn,'" Jimmy said sarcastically, making air quotes, "up the mountain. Whatever that means."

Candice chuckled. "A newbie, I think."

"I know these mountains, too. I know I've been gone for a while, but I grew up here. Did Stu?"

"No. I believe Stu is from Canmore. So, still the mountains, just different ones."

"Exactly." Jimmy shook his head. "But you're the boss lady, too, and I suppose he wants the 'greenhorn' to go with the boss lady."

"Stop air-quoting 'greenhorn,'" Candice said, laughing. "You look like a chicken when you do that."

Jimmy cocked an eyebrow. "How is that?"

"You stick out your neck like a chicken."

"Okay then. You sure you're over that concussion?" He was grinning, his eyes twinkling.

"Pretty sure." She climbed into the passenger seat and buckled up while Jimmy climbed into the driver's side. They drove across town and Candice stayed in the car while Jimmy ran inside to grab Marcus and Marcus's bag. It was just an hour's drive to Hinton, but they would need provisions, especially for a toddler. She may not have kids, but she knew that they required a lot of stuff.

Stuff that she wished she had.

Yes, she had big aspirations to become a surgeon, but she also wanted a family. She wanted a couple of kids.

Jimmy came out of the house with a diaper bag slung over his shoulder and Marcus in his arms.

Jimmy opened the back door and set Marcus down in his car seat.

"Hi, Marcus!" Candice said, smiling at the little boy.

Marcus was drinking out of his sippy cup, but he smiled behind it, his eyes crinkling and twinkling with recognition. Jimmy finished strapping in Marcus and then passed the diaper bag to Candice over the seat.

"Here, you better man the bag. There's snacks and stuff in there and if I left it back here with him he'd lay waste to it. Wouldn't you, Marcus?" Jimmy teased his son, who laughed at him from behind his cup.

Jimmy finished making sure that Marcus had what he needed and then climbed into the front seat.

"You got everything?" Candice asked.

"Yes. And a list from my mom. There's some stuff she wants us to pick up for the party. It's all in the diaper bag. As well as some extra things to keep him occupied, but honestly, he's due for a nap so hopefully he'll sleep on the way to Hinton and then be ready to go when we get to the superstore."

"Does he sleep well in the car?" Candice asked.

"He does. When we drove from Toronto back home, my mom came with us. She flew to Toronto and helped me pack up what little we had into the trailer I rented and then we made the trip out west together. She kept Marcus busy in the back and I was able to focus on driving. When I moved back it was spring and there were still parts of northern Ontario and the prairies that were getting late snowfalls."

"Yeah, it was a weird winter," she said.

"And driving around Lake Superior with a trailer and a baby was no picnic. I was glad my mom was able to help, but really, she'd do anything for Marcus. If it was just me, she'd make me fend for myself," he quipped.

"That's not true and you know it."

He nodded. "Yes. I'm joking. I would've thought that in the past, but Marcus has really opened up my eyes, and though it's still not perfect, my relationship with my parents is better than it's ever been before. I'm glad they have a good relationship with Marcus."

Candice chuckled. "Your mom sure does love him."

"And I don't?" Jimmy teased.

"You do. That's not what I meant."

"I know what you meant. And, yeah, it's true. Marcus is the light of her life."

As they pulled out of town, leaving Jasper behind them, Marcus started to drift off to sleep, and held tight to his little sippy cup full of water. Candice smiled at him.

"He really is cute," she said.

"I think so." Jimmy grinned at her.

"Do you think he'll sleep the whole way there?" Candice asked.

"He should."

"I'll never understand how little kids can sleep in such odd positions."

Jimmy chuckled. "I think adults can, too. I mean I remember sleeping in some crummy, tight spaces when I was a teen. Especially after a bush party."

Candice winced. "Yeah, I remember some of those bush parties. You and Logan really were the worst influences."

"What? It gave you an appreciation of nature, I bet." He winked at her and she laughed.

"I suppose it did. It's why I love Jasper so much."

And that was why Chad had left her. He didn't want to spend his life in Jasper. He didn't want to take care of her father when he got sick.

He didn't want a family.

And truth be told, he was never much of an outdoors person. She should've seen it earlier, but she hadn't. She had met him in university when her family members were all alive and well, and he had dazzled her with his charm. And then she'd lost Logan, and her mom, and her dad had closed in on himself a bit, so she'd clung to Chad like a lifeline because she didn't want to be alone.

"That's probably why my marriage ended," she said quietly.

"Yeah, you never really told me about…what was his name?" Jimmy asked.

"Chad."

"That's a horrible name." Jimmy made a face. "Who names their kid Chad?"

"Chad is not a horrible name. Our marriage didn't end because of his name."

"Fine. So then why did it end?"

"We wanted different things. He didn't want to stay in Jasper, unless we were going to upgrade to a condo or a lodge where we could ski and host parties. Fancy parties. He didn't want to stay and help take care of my dad when he first got sick. He also really detested the outdoors. unless it was clean, sanitary and socially acceptable."

Jimmy cocked an eyebrow. "What did you see in him?"

"He was nice. We had a good time when we met in college. I loved him and we both were focused on medicine. And to be fair, he was supportive of me when Logan was killed and my mom started going downhill, but he wanted to go back to school. He wanted to be a doctor. He wanted a life in the big city and I wanted to stay in Jasper."

"You really wanted to stay in Jasper?" he asked.

"I did." She smiled. "It was hard to give up medical school. It hurt, but it was the right thing to do at the time. I love Jasper. Chad didn't, so he left."

And it had hurt more than she had expected. She thought she'd built walls to protect herself, but when Chad left those walls had crumbled more easily than she could have imagined. She had barely survived Jimmy leaving and that second abandonment forced her to realize that the only way to protect herself was by never letting anyone close in the first place. So she'd closed off her heart, thrown herself into looking after her dad, and after that into work, and she had been just fine.

Until Jimmy came back and upset her carefully ordered existence.

"Since I told you about Chad, why don't you tell me about Marcus's mom. You told me she passed away."

"She did," Jimmy sighed. "I met her after I got back from Germany. She had served, too, and she had some problems with PTSD that she never dealt with. I couldn't see it at the time—I was still coming to terms with what had happened with Logan—and we grew close and got together one night. Then she left. I didn't love her. I cared for her, she was my friend, but I wouldn't call it love. Then, six months after Marcus was born, he was left on my doorstep. She couldn't handle it. It broke me not to know about him until six months later, but still I tried to get her help with her PTSD. She didn't want it, though, and there was nothing further I could do."

"That's too bad." She felt even worse that she hadn't told him sooner about their baby. That it had been kept from him for so long.

Jimmy nodded. "It sucked. She had no one, and one night she drank too much…"

"I'm sorry. And I'm sorry that Marcus won't know his mother."

Jimmy gave a sad smile. "Yeah, me, too. I did manage to locate her father, but he didn't want anything to do with Marcus, or me, for that matter, but he did give me a picture of Jennifer in her uniform. So I have that put away for when Marcus wants to learn about his mother."

"Have you ever thought about getting married?"

"Nope. Never thought about it," Jimmy said quickly. "All I've been focused on is moving back to Jasper to give him a great place to grow up and to give him the chance to be close to his grandparents. I'm trying to rebuild my life after a rough couple of years. Marriage is the last thing on my mind."

Candice didn't know why she was disappointed when he said that.

She certainly wasn't looking to get married again, but the way he so quickly dismissed the idea gave her an unexpected surge of sadness—for him and for Marcus. They deserved all the happiness in the world. She couldn't give it to them—she couldn't risk her heart again, wouldn't put herself in that position—but she wanted it so badly for them both.

The rest of the hour-long drive to Hinton was unremarkable. She was used to this stretch of road and she never really tired of just staring out the window at the mountains, trees, rocks and occasional animals.

It was a bright, sunny and clear day.

The water sparkled, flashing a brilliant blue from the mineral runoff and the springs underneath that fed the various lakes.

Marcus continued his nap and only woke up once before Jimmy pulled into the parking lot of the superstore, where they could grab everything they needed from Liena's list and where Candice could find Marcus a birthday present.

Jimmy parked and they got of the car, Candice grabbing her purse and the diaper bag. Jimmy got Marcus out, locked the car and carried him over to a shopping cart, sitting him down in the baby seat.

"I'm going to have to change him when we get inside," Jimmy remarked. "He's quite ripe."

Candice laughed and put the diaper bag in the cart. "It'll give me a chance to pick out a present for him without him noticing."

"He won't remember, even if you pick it out right in front of him. As long as you wrap it in garish-colored paper or a giant box he can destroy, he'll be happy. This is what I've learned about kids since Marcus turned one—much like cats, kids like playing with the box itself a lot more than what's inside the box."

Candice laughed. "Okay then, but we'll have to distract him with something small so he won't cry when I take away the present to wrap it up for him."

"This is true. We'll have to get some ice cream!"

Marcus squealed and clapped his hands. "Ice cweam!"

"That's right," Jimmy said. "Ice cream, but first shopping for Năinai and then ice cream. Okay, buddy?"

Marcus nodded and then grinned at Candice. "Ice cweam, Candy!"

"That's right!" And her heart melted as Marcus giggled and squirmed in the shopping-cart seat. He was so excited about the prospect of ice cream—it was adorable.

"Now you know why I bring extra clothes," Jimmy said.

"I have friends who have kids. I get it."

Once they got in the store Jimmy picked up Marcus and took him to get changed while Candice shopped for the stuff on Liena's list.

Jimmy and Marcus came back a few moments later, Jimmy holding Marcus's tiny, chubby hand in his as Marcus toddled beside his tall father.

Her heart skipped a beat as she saw them.

Marcus smiled and waved and she couldn't help but smile and wave back at him. Then he pulled free of his father's hand and ran toward her, his chubby little legs barely supporting his body as he ran down the aisle, squealing and laughing.

Candice kneeled down and he ran into her arms, throwing his arms around her neck and hugging her—he wanted her to pick him up. Her heart swelled and she completely melted, holding him in her arms as she stood.

Jimmy looked a bit shocked as he approached her. "I have never seen him warm up to someone so fast before."

"Well, that's because he knows that Candy rocks. Right, Marcus?"

Marcus nodded.

Candice placed him in the cart and he happily squirmed as she pushed the cart up and down the aisles.

This felt like how it always should have been. It made her happy and yet it scared her. Her heart was slipping into Jimmy's hands again.

And she hated that it felt so right.

That she wanted it to be right.

They finished up their shopping after Candice found a present for Marcus and they distracted him with an ice-cream cone when they were leaving the superstore. He was happily making a mess while they loaded up the back of Jimmy's car with everything that would be needed for the birthday party in a few days.

"It's a beautiful day," Candice remarked. It was sunny, warm and clear. There would be so many people out on the mountain and her mind immediately went to what was happening at work.

"Where are you?" Jimmy asked as he kneeled down and wiped off Marcus's sticky hands.

"What do you mean?" she asked. "I'm here."

"You were thinking about work, weren't you?" Jimmy teased.

"Maybe. The park will be packed. There will be a lot of people out and about."

"That's pretty pathetic you're thinking about all the rescues you could be doing because there will be more people in the park." He winked at her and put Marcus back in his car seat.

"It's not that!"

"No?" he asked.

"No. Well, it's partly that, but I've been running Mountain Rescue for three years and I'm wondering how they're getting along without me."

"It'll be okay. Stu is good."

She shot him a dirty look. "What?"

He threw up his hands. "You're better. Obviously, boss."

Candice sighed. "It'll be good to get back next week and I'm looking forward to getting out on the trail."

"Actually, I'm looking forward to that, too. It's been a long time since I did a backcountry hike."

"Well, we're going to do the Skyline Trail. It's one of the busiest backcountry trails, but the most problematic. It's going to be a pain hiking with all that emergency climbing gear. It might be needed, but hopefully not."

"Let's hope not. So what do you say we get some lunch and make our way down to the Beaver Boardwalk and walk some of it? See if we can see some beavers."

"That sounds fun."

It had been a long time since she'd gone walking along the boardwalk through the wetlands. Actually, she couldn't even remember the last time she'd been down there. When she came to Hinton, she was usually on a mission to get her groceries and leave.

This would be nice.

They picked up some sandwiches and a grilled cheese for Marcus, then drove to the trail and parked. They walked for a bit, letting Marcus stretch his legs along the boardwalk, which meant they had to stop every few minutes so that the boy could squat down and stare at the water and the marsh.

It was adorable.

They didn't walk too far before they found a nice picnic spot near Maxwell Lake and sat down to eat.

Marcus couldn't walk the length of the trail and neither could Candice. Her ankle was bothering her a bit, but she was glad for the stretch. She would make sure to ice and elevate it tonight.

"I forgot about this place," she said. "My parents used to bring Logan and I here when we were younger. I don't know how many times Logan threatened to feed me to the beavers."

Jimmy chuckled.

"Logan liked to bring his dates here to make out."

"Gross."

"What?" Jimmy asked.

"It's bad enough I had to see my brother streak from time to time, but I really don't need to know about where he brought girls to score."

Jimmy chuckled. "Sorry."

"Why did he bring them to a swamp?"

"Wetlands," Jimmy corrected, grinning at her. "And I thought you didn't want to know. I thought it was gross."

She rolled her eyes. "It is, but still I'm curious about the choice of destination."

Jimmy shrugged. "It's quiet here and pretty. It's different from the river or the mountains, I suppose. This wasn't his only spot."

"Yeah. I'm good." She smiled, thinking of her brother. He'd been so well-liked by everyone. She missed him. He was the best big brother a girl could have had—even if he was a complete contrast to her—and it seemed unfair that his life had been cut so short.

"I didn't bring girls here," Jimmy said. "I was too classy."

"Where did you bring girls?" She couldn't believe she was asking him this.

Jimmy shrugged. "Usually to the river, but honestly I never really had the same amount of girls that Logan had. There was the odd one or two, but not really."

"I find that hard to believe," she said.

"It's true."

"You always had some girl on your arm."

His gaze was intense, and it made her pulse quicken. "Just because the girls were on my arm doesn't mean anything happened. There was only ever one girl I wanted to take out. You were my first, too, Candice."

Her cheeks heated. "I know."

Her heart was hammering against her chest, feeling like it was going burst out.

"You were the only one I ever wanted," he whispered.

She leaned forward, wanting to ask him so many things, but they were interrupted by a loud screech.

"Daddy, I made a mess," Marcus shouted.

Jimmy broke their shared gaze and looked

down at his son. "You sure did, buddy. That's a lot of ketchup."

Candice leaned over and tried not to laugh. "Oh, my. Yeah that is."

"I'm going to take him to the restroom and clean him up." Jimmy picked up the diaper bag.

"I'll clean up here. You done with your lunch, Marcus?" Candice asked.

"Yes, Candy. I done."

"Oh, good."

Jimmy took Marcus by the hand and Candice watched the two of them walk away. Her heart skipped a beat again.

You can have this.

All she had to do was not be so afraid and take the plunge, but she was scared of being hurt and losing it all.

"You have a beautiful family there."

Candice spun around to see an elderly couple walking past the picnic table.

"Pardon?" Candice asked, shocked.

The elderly woman smiled. "Your family. You have a beautiful family. How old is the little boy?"

"He'll be two soon," Candice answered stunned.

"Ah, the terrible twos. Although not so terrible. Enjoy it." The elderly woman smiled and continued on her way with her husband.

Candice stood there for a few moments, her hands full of garbage. She didn't correct the older woman and she should have.

Jimmy and Marcus were not her family.

But she wanted them to be. If only she was brave enough to take the chance.

CHAPTER TEN

THE RIDE HOME was quiet, with Marcus sleeping in the backseat, completely played out. Jimmy looked over at Candice and even she was dozing, her head resting against the door.

It brought a smile to his face as he took his time and made his way back to Jasper.

He really didn't want this moment to end.

It was peaceful.

And it felt right.

All he'd ever wanted was Candice.

Nothing about that had changed.

After he had cleaned up Marcus from the ketchup incident, they'd strolled around the boardwalk for a while and then found a park so that Marcus could run around. It was close to dinner and they had had a quick bite to eat and then made their way back to Jasper.

It was only six o'clock in the evening, but it had been a long day for both Marcus and Candice. He was surprised Candice had managed to make it so long through her first real outing after her accident.

He slowed down as they approached the park gate and Candice woke up.

"Are we home?" she asked.

"No, we just made it to the gate. You can go back to sleep if you want."

She winced. "I don't think that I can. It's not very comfortable sleeping in a car, to be honest."

"No. I know."

Jimmy showed their pass at the gate. There was hardly anyone on the road—it was just them, the mountains and an odd goat that had ambled down to eat grass along the highway.

"That was a good day," Candice sighed.

"It was."

She looked back at Marcus. "He's fast asleep."

"Car rides are magic for him." Jimmy laughed and then frowned at something he saw in the distance—flashing four-ways and a woman waving her arms frantically from the shoulder, where there was a small dirt road that led to one of the recreation areas off the Yellowhead Highway.

"What's going on here?" Jimmy murmured. He pulled off the road and parked the car close to the woman's van, then rolled down his window as the woman lurched over, her hand on her very pregnant belly.

"Thank God," the woman whispered breathlessly. "I need help."

"Sure. What's wrong?" Jimmy asked, shutting off the ignition.

"My husband, he was driving and he just passed out! I don't know what happened. I had to steer the car the best I could and managed to pull off here, but he's not waking up."

"Have you called an ambulance?" Jimmy asked calmly.

She shook her head, trembling. "No. I didn't… think."

"It's okay. We've got it and I'm a paramedic. I can help." Jimmy turned to Candice, who was already pulling out her phone and calling emergency services from Hinton, since it was closer to where they were, between Jasper and Hinton. "Stay with Marcus."

Candice nodded and took the keys from him as she gave their coordinates to the first responders in Hinton.

Jimmy got out of the car and grabbed his medical kit from the trunk. He pulled on his gloves and followed the terrified woman to her van.

"What's his name?" Jimmy asked.

"Steve," she whispered.

"And what's yours?" Jimmy asked as he reached in and felt for a pulse.

"Mary."

"Mary, I'm going to get your husband out of the van and I'm going to check his airways, okay?" Jimmy was trying not to alarm her, but there was a faint, sluggish pulse. The cause of Steve's unconsciousness could be as simple as low blood sugar or as serious as a stroke. He needed to get Steve on his back so he could check his airways and elevate his legs.

Candice got out of the car. The windows had been opened and the doors were locked, so Marcus was safe, asleep and close by.

"Ambulance is on its way," Candice said. "Thirty minutes out."

Jimmy nodded. He moved and extracted Steve from the front seat, lying him on the ground. He positioned Steve on his back and then loosened his belt and unbuttoned his shirt a bit—anything to keep restrictions of blood flow to a minimum.

He then checked to see if anything was blocking the airway, it wasn't.

"Steve? Can you hear me?" Jimmy asked as he checked the ABCs, but there was no response. He raised Steve's legs at least twelve inches off the ground, hoping for some response, but there was none.

Dammit.

He was going to have to do CPR. He looked at Candice and shook his head. Candice nodded in silent response and moved to Mary, to keep her occupied.

"Mary, I'm Candice and I'm a first responder. Can you tell me what happened?"

"He was driving me to the hospital. My water broke about an hour ago." Mary winced and breathed deep.

"You're in labor?" Candice asked, stunned.

Jimmy whipped his head around from where he was doing CPR. "She's in labor?"

"How far apart are your contractions, Mary?"

Mary shrugged. "I don't know, less than a minute. This is my fourth baby."

"Candice, you need to get the emergency blanket out of my trunk and get Mary set up in the back of her van. Okay?"

Candice nodded and moved quickly. She opened the hatch of Mary's van and set up the emergency solar blanket, then had Mary sit down on it.

"Do you feel any pressure, Mary? Any urgency to push?" Candice asked.

"Oh, yeah. I wasn't paying attention before… but I feel it." Mary winced again. "I just want to push."

Candice grabbed gloves from Jimmy's vehicle while he continued his compressions.

"I've never delivered a baby," she said under her breath.

"You can do this. This is her fourth, remember your first aid and your basic training," he said. There was no way they could switch. Jimmy had to keep up with compressions, and with Candice just getting over a concussion, there was no way she'd be able to keep up with the CPR.

Candice nodded and he watched her make her way back to Mary while he kept the CPR going on Steve. He was hoping he'd hear that sweet sound of a siren soon.

"The baby is crowning," Candice called out.

Come on, Steve. Wake up and see your baby being born.

That was when he heard Steve gasp.

Jimmy rolled him on his side. "Breathe for me. Breathe."

He finally heard a siren in the distance and he breathed a sigh of relief.

"You're okay, Steve. You're okay. I'm Jimmy Liu, a paramedic. You were unconscious."

"Mary?" Steve croaked.

"She's okay," Jimmy reassured him as the ambulance pulled up, its sirens off, but with the lights flashing. Jimmy glanced over and Marcus was still out like a light.

The doors of the ambulance opened and Jimmy spoke with the paramedics, giving them all the information he'd gathered while examining Steve.

"Jimmy, I need your help!" Candice called out.

"We've got this," the paramedic said.

Jimmy nodded and headed over to help Candice.

"The baby is not coming. A shoulder might be stuck," Candice said calmly.

"Okay. We need to get Mary into the McRoberts maneuver." Jimmy climbed in behind Mary. "Mary, I need you to bring your legs up toward your tummy. Candice, try to move the baby to free the shoulder."

Candice nodded, but he could briefly see the concern in her eye.

Jimmy sat behind Mary and helped hold her legs. If this didn't work during the next contraction, he'd push on her belly.

"Okay, Mary, when you feel the next contraction, push!" Jimmy ordered.

Mary cried out and Candice moved the baby gently. That was all it took and the baby was quickly delivered. Candice held the infant in her gloved hands.

"It's a girl!" Candice said, her voice shaking.

The baby let out a cry and Jimmy congratulated Mary as Candice laid the baby down on her belly. They wouldn't cut the cord here in the back of the van.

A second ambulance pulled up and paramedics came rushing over. Jimmy climbed out of the back of the van and noticed that Marcus was awake, staring at the lights.

Candice covered Mary and the baby with another blanket, and she seemed to be gazing at the happy mom and healthy baby with longing.

It caused a twinge of longing in him, too, and made him pause, thinking about the baby they had lost. It broke his heart that he never got to share in the joy of the pregnancy with Candice, hadn't been there to comfort her in the sadness of the loss. They'd never met their son or daughter, never have the chance to watch their child grow. The thoughts and emotions threatened to overwhelm him, but he forced himself back into the present moment. His son needed him. And, right now, he really needed his son.

He removed his gloves and disposed of them in one of the biomedical waste containers the ambulance had. He sanitized his hands, then got Marcus, lifting his little boy out of the car and holding him tight.

"Daddy, look!"

"I know, right, buddy?" Jimmy said, kissing him.

Mary was being put on a stretcher with the baby and Candice was cleaning up and giving the paramedics information on the birth.

She came over and shut the back door of Mary's van, making sure it was secure.

"We have to wait for the tow truck," Candice said. "I have all their information."

Jimmy nodded.

"Candy, look!" Marcus said, pointing to the ambulances.

"I know!" Candice smiled. "There's a tow truck coming soon, too!"

Marcus made a face, his eyes wide, as Jimmy looked at him.

"Sounds fun, right, buddy?" Jimmy asked.

Marcus nodded. "I sit."

"Okay." He set Marcus back in the back seat with his toys and a cup of juice, making himself comfortable to wait it out, "reading" a book that was upside down.

Jimmy sighed and leaned against the car, Candice next to him as they watched the ambulances pull off the side road and head out onto the highway, back to Hinton.

"That was…something," Candice said, laughing nervously.

"It was." Jimmy smiled down at her. "You did a good job."

"That was the first time I delivered a baby."

"Your first time?" he asked. "I would've never guessed it."

"Yeah, you don't get many pregnant women up on the mountain passes."

"You did a good job for your first time."

"Thanks." She nodded. "So did you, knowing that move to help the baby and helping the father."

"You kept your calm, too. We make a good team."

A strange look passed on her face. "Yes. We do."

"But what?" he asked.

"Well, helping Mary deliver that baby just makes me want to go back to school even more. I mean, what's keeping me here, really? What's stopping me from packing up and going? There's nothing for me in Jasper anymore…is there?"

Jimmy's heart sunk down to the soles of his feet.

You can't be the one thing that holds her back.

"Yeah. You should do that." He turned and

looked down the highway, watching as the tow truck finally came into view.

"I'll give the driver the information and then we can head back to Jasper." Candice walked away and Jimmy sighed.

He couldn't be selfish. She should go back to school and follow her dreams. She was smart and had a clear, calm presence. She would make an amazing doctor. Look at how well she'd handled unexpectedly having to deliver a baby. He had been so proud of her in that moment.

He couldn't hold her back from seeing what she was truly capable of.

Even if he wanted her to stay with him more than anything in the world.

CHAPTER ELEVEN

"ANSWER THE DOOR, JIMMY!" Liena shouted from the kitchen.

"Okay." Jimmy really hoped his mother's shouting didn't wake up Marcus. They weren't quite ready for his birthday party. At least the couple of other kids who were invited—mostly neighborhood families his parents knew—hadn't arrived yet, so it was still pretty quiet.

He was so behind schedule.

He opened the door and was relieved to see Candice standing there.

Jimmy hadn't seen her in a couple of days, not since they went to Hinton.

He'd been keeping his distance since she mentioned wanting to go back to school, but it was such a relief to see her.

He'd missed her and she looked so nice. Her dark hair was tied back and she was wearing a pretty floral blouse and denim skirt. It was summery and casual, and she looked so beautiful. It was all he could do not to stare at her in appreciation.

"Thank God it's you," he said in exasperation, the balloon he'd been trying to hold closed deflating with a horrible sound.

Candice watched the balloon zoom out of his hand and across the room. "Problems?"

"Marcus didn't sleep last night. I had to attend a rescue and I'm behind on blowing up balloons. It's not going well."

"Well, your mom called me and asked me to come early." Candice handed him a brightly colored package. "For Marcus."

"Thanks. I wonder what it could be," he quipped and then stepped aside to let her in. "How have you been?"

"I'm good," she said quickly, barely looking at him.

Yep. It was definitely awkward.

"You sure?" he asked.

She looked at him like he was crazy. "Why wouldn't I be sure?"

"You just seem on edge," Jimmy said, closing the door.

"If you must know, I am anxious about returning to work tomorrow. I'm worried about what's waiting for me and how much paperwork there's going to be."

"Well," he finally said, "I could use your

help decorating. Hopefully that will take your mind off work and the horrible mess that Stu made."

He was teasing, hoping to bring levity to the situation. Hoping to get a rise out of her and take their relationship back to the way it was.

What relationship?

He didn't have a relationship with her and he had to remind himself of that.

"Sounds good."

His mother came out of the kitchen and smiled. "Candice, I'm so glad you're here!"

"Glad to be here, Mrs. Liu."

"Liena," his mother said. "Can you come help me finish decorating the cake?"

"Of course." Candice moved past him to the kitchen.

"Mom, she's helping me with balloons," Jimmy protested.

His mother looked at him. "I don't know why you're struggling with this—you're full of enough hot air."

His father, who was sitting in the living room doing nothing but reading a newspaper, laughed.

Jimmy glared at him. "You know, you could help, Pop."

His father raised his paper higher and said, "You're doing a fine job, son."

Jimmy rolled his eyes and went back to blowing up balloons, trying to rush through the decorating he was doing so that he could speak to Candice before the rest of the guests arrived. He watched her in the kitchen with his mother, helping get the food ready for their neighbors, and it warmed his heart to see Candice working so well with his mother.

She wanted to go back to school and he had to let her.

It was her dream.

He couldn't hold her back.

He had to let her go.

Again.

When Marcus woke up, Jimmy's father scooted upstairs to get him while Jimmy finished the last touches on the decorations inside as the first of the guests arrived.

He didn't think that this would be so much work, but Marcus had made friends with a few of the toddlers in the neighborhood and his parents had insisted on giving Marcus a proper birthday, even though Jimmy couldn't remember his parents ever giving him a birthday as elaborate as this. He'd get a cake and Logan would come over, but it would be brief.

And usually it was just his mom who would be there, as his dad had to run the motel.

Jimmy didn't know who half these people were, but they knew his parents and Marcus, and several of them seemed to know Candice.

As Jimmy navigated the crowd, he watched Candice from a distance.

He couldn't help himself.

And the more he watched her, the more he wanted her.

His blood heated as he thought of their kiss before her accident. It was all he could think about these days. In fact, he hadn't stopped thinking about her since he'd first returned to Jasper and run in to her again. She was like a ghost coming back to haunt him.

Taunt him.

"It's time to sing 'Happy Birthday' to the birthday boy," his mother said, interrupting his troubling train of thought.

"Of course," Jimmy said, shaking thoughts of Candice from his head.

He had to focus on his son.

He found Marcus running around with a couple of kids in the backyard. Candice was also outside, talking with one of his neighbors—another single father, about their age—and a pang of jealously hit him.

Focus.

Jimmy picked up Marcus. "Time for cake!"

Marcus clapped his hands and Jimmy sat down with him at the picnic table.

His mother came out of the house carrying a cake in the shape of the ugliest dog Jimmy had ever seen, but it made Marcus happy and everyone sang "Happy Birthday."

Marcus squealed in delight, and with his help, they blew out the candle and his mom took pictures, blinding them all.

"Come to Yéye," his father said, holding out his hands. "We'll have cake together."

Jimmy handed over Marcus to his dad while his mother began cutting the cake. Looking around, he noticed that Candice had headed inside, so he got up to follow her. It was much quieter inside.

"You need help?" he asked.

Candice jumped, startled. "Why did you sneak up on me like that?"

"Sorry. I didn't mean to."

"I'm trying to find the ice-cream bowls your mom said were in here. I found the tray and the spoons, but not the paper bowls."

"They're in the dining room." Jimmy headed into the dining room to grab them from the hutch, where his mother had squirrelled away party stuff. "Here they are."

"Great." Candice took the bag of paper bowls from him.

"Are you avoiding me?" he asked.

"What?" she asked, shocked.

"You've been acting weird."

"I don't know what you're talking about. You've been avoiding me!"

Jimmy shut the door to the dining room so they'd have some privacy.

"I'm not avoiding you." Only that was a lie. He was.

"Really?" she asked, unconvinced. She took a step closer to him.

"I've been busy."

"Something changed after that rescue," she said.

"Nothing has changed except…" His pulse was thundering in his ears. All he wanted was her. All he could think of was that kiss they shared.

"What, Jimmy?" she asked, a blush in her cheeks. "What's wrong?"

"Candice." And before he could think rationally about where they were or why it was a bad idea, he pulled her into his arms and kissed her, like he'd wanted to ever since the last time he'd kissed her.

The bag of paper bowls dropped to the floor and her arms were around him. All he could think about were her lips on his. His blood was singing and his body burned with desire for her.

He wanted her.

Only her.

He wanted to taste her, to touch every inch of her.

He wanted to be lost in her kisses.

"Candice? Where's the ice cream?" his mother called out.

Candice broke the kiss. "That shouldn't have happened. I'm your boss... I... That shouldn't have happened."

She picked up the package of bowls and opened the door, scurrying out of the room, leaving Jimmy standing there, stunned.

He shouldn't have kissed her. He didn't know what he was thinking and he was angry at himself.

Hadn't he convinced himself that he wasn't going to hold her back? That he wasn't going to ruin her dreams? He shouldn't have kissed her. He had to put a stop to this once and for all.

Because the only dreams that he was willing to ruin were his own.

Candice couldn't get that kiss out of her head.

The first one she'd thought about a lot, but this one was heated. Urgent. Her body still thrummed with need.

She couldn't believe that she had lost control like that.

It had been so hot.

She had to get control of herself, had to figure out what she wanted. Yes, she wanted to go back to school, but she wanted Jimmy, too. She wanted both him and Marcus in her life, but could she put her heart on the line again? Could she walk away from the guarantees of medicine for the uncertainty of Jimmy's love? She was so scared of being hurt, of losing it all, of ending up alone, again.

After Marcus had opened his gifts, she left discreetly, telling Liena she had a headache and saying nothing to Jimmy.

She had to put distance between them. She had to think.

When she returned to work the next day, she had a lot of paperwork waiting for her, so she spent her time doing that, because she wasn't cleared to fly quite yet and she didn't want to go out into the field until she did her round on the Skyline Trail.

Stu kept Jimmy busy so they didn't have to say much to each other.

Which was perfect.

Was it?

She was missing him. Missing their talks.

Before he'd come back into her life, she'd been lonely, but used to it. Now, she felt that absence, that ache of isolation, too keenly.

So she threw herself into her paperwork, hoping it would take her mind off everything.

It didn't.

Candice knew that she was fooling herself. Especially as they were getting ready to go on their backcountry round. She was going to have to make amends.

She worried her bottom lip and rubbed her temples before pushing the intercom to the ambulance bay.

"Jimmy, can you come to my office?"

"Sure thing, boss."

She cringed at him calling her *boss*.

No, this was better. This was normal.

Only a part of her couldn't help but wonder, was it?

Jimmy knocked and entered her office.

"You wanted to see me?" he asked. She could tell he was uncomfortable, too.

He looks so good in his uniform.

"Tomorrow, you ready for our backcountry trip?" she asked.

"I am. I packed a basic medical kit."

"Most of the injuries, if we encounter any, are minor. Major rescues are usually called in and we do a helicopter rescue if we can.

The Skyline Trail is well populated and slots of time, with the number of hikers all on, always fill up."

He nodded. "I remember."

"Stu will drop us off at the Maligne trailhead and we'll walk toward Signal Mountain before being picked up again."

"You're not going the opposite way?" he asked.

"No, I like to go that way because starting at Maligne, you've already gained a lot of elevation and can go downhill."

He smiled. "That sounds smart."

"Look, I know that things have been weird—"

"I know. And it was my fault. I'm sorry for what happened. I want you to know it won't happen again. I want to be friends, Candice."

She knew it was for the best, but still felt the stab of disappointment, and was angry at herself for being disappointed. She shouldn't care. She wouldn't care. If he could walk away, then so could she. "I want that, too."

"Good." Jimmy nodded. "Do you need me for anything else?"

"No. I'll meet you here tomorrow morning about seven a.m., that way we can get a start on the trail and get to the Snowbowl site in the first day."

"Sounds good. I'll see you bright and early tomorrow." Jimmy left her office and she released the breath that she hadn't known that she was holding.

It was better this way.

Was it really though?

She shook her head, trying to dispel the niggling thought in her mind. Trying to ignore the voice in her head telling her to take a chance on Jimmy Liu, like she wanted to.

It was a want that terrified her. Terrified her of being hurt again. After Jimmy, and then Chad, she couldn't handle another broken heart.

It was going to be a long four days indeed.

CHAPTER TWELVE

S<small>TU DROVE THEM</small> out to the Maligne trailhead.
They weren't the only hikers that were about
to start on their journey and there were already
other hikers on the various points of the trail,
judging by the way the parking lot was full.

Every slot of the Skyline Trail had been
booked for July and August, while Septem-
ber and October were almost full, too. It was
one of the most popular backcountry hikes in
Jasper so you had to claim your spot well in
advance and there were always hikers waiting
in town to see if someone canceled.

There was one lodge at the halfway point
of the trail that catered to people who had the
money to pay for a night or two of all-inclusive
lodging and, thankfully, they were going to
stay at the lodge for one night, because it was
included in their rounds. They wouldn't reach
the lodge until their second night, though, so
they'd be camping out tonight.

She had her list of everyone that should be on the trail and she knew what to do if they found someone on the trail who shouldn't be there, though she hoped that they wouldn't have that problem.

Their plan was to get to the Snowbowl campground before nightfall, and the ride to the trailhead had been quiet, with Jimmy going through his pack and Candice trying not to think about everything she was feeling and the fact it would be just be the two of them out there.

At least they would have their work.

That would distract her.

You're here to do your job and train Jimmy. That's it. After this, you won't have to hike the trail with him ever again if you don't want to.

Stu parked the truck. "Got everything you need, Lavoie?"

Candice nodded. "And I have my satellite phone ready in case we have to call in a helicopter. Hopefully we won't."

Stu nodded. "When I did the Tonquin trail you were supposed to do, we didn't encounter anything really worrisome, just some bog foot from walking too long in wet gear and minor injuries."

"Let's hope we have the same luck," Jimmy said from the back.

"Thanks, Stu. See you at Signal Mountain in four days," Candice said.

Stu nodded and Candice climbed out of the truck. She grabbed her gear and slipped it on her back. Jimmy clipped his pack on and handed Candice her walking poles. With all the gear they were carrying and her ankle just recovered, she was happy to have the walking poles for support.

Stu drove out of the packed parking lot with a wave.

"It's busy here," Jimmy remarked.

"It is. It's one of the most popular trails. That being said, there won't be a ton of people on it. Or shouldn't be. I'm hoping we don't have to issue fines."

"Let's hope not."

They made their way to start of the trailhead, with Candice leading the climb, as she'd done this route before. She liked hiking the Skyline Trail and it was a good hike to test Jimmy on, even though she knew that he and her brother had done this hike on their own before.

Still, it had been some time since Jimmy had been here and she wondered if he'd struggle with the elevation climb after spending so much time away from Jasper. She wondered if he had any residual pain in his legs or hip that would affect his hiking. It had been five years since his injuries, but it was possible the pain still flared up now and again, especially as he'd said it took him a year to recover, but so far he was doing well.

As they kept walking, she kept turning around to check on him, but he was keeping up with her.

After an hour and a half of hiking, they came to the Evelyn Creek campsite.

"We didn't hike very far," Jimmy said as they sat down on a picnic table.

"No, we'll stay here for half an hour, check on the campers that are here or come through and fill our water bottles. Then we'll continue on."

Jimmy nodded and set down his pack. "I always thought it was strange to have a campsite so close to the trailhead."

"Well, it depends which way you're coming and how late you started. Some people start from Signal Mountain and end up at Maligne. Personally, I like this way better."

He nodded and then sat down next to her on the picnic table. "How is your ankle?"

"It's fine." It ached a bit, but she didn't want to worry him and it was nothing she couldn't deal with. She had a tensor bandage to wrap it tonight, when they got to the Snowbowl campsite.

And she was looking forward to getting to the lodge near the Curator campground tomorrow night.

Even just to have a bed for one night would be great.

"Do you want me to make the rounds and see if anyone is camping?"

"Sure. I'll stay here and watch the trail."

Jimmy nodded and slipped off the picnic table to check the campsite. She seriously doubted anyone would be there. If anyone was, they'd likely left and started off early up the trail. Still, they had to make their rounds.

Jimmy came jogging back. "There's a camper with a swollen hand. Probably a sprain, but I said I would look at it."

"Okay." Candice jumped down off the picnic table. "Let's go."

They picked up their packs and made it down to the hiker's campsite.

Candice checked to make sure he had a permit and he did. He told them he was on his way down the trail, having started at Signal Mountain. He planned to finish a bit early, but slipped and fell, spraining his hand the previous night, so instead of finishing early he spent his last night camping and was having a hard time packing up his gear. Joshua Mooney was a young man from Jasper and liked to do the Skyline at least once a year.

Jimmy checked out his hand.

"Do you have someone picking you up at Maligne?" Candice asked. "You can't drive with that hand."

"Yeah. I have my satellite phone to call my ride. Told them I'd be down there in a couple of hours, but I'm having issues packing up and getting out of here."

"We can help," Candice said.

"You might have a dislocated knuckle," Jimmy said. "Once you get picked up you should head to the hospital in Jasper and get it checked out. I'll wrap it, but you definitely need an X-ray and some splints."

"Thanks," Joshua said. "This is the first time I've hurt myself on a trail. Or hurt myself this bad. Glad you guys came by."

"Glad to help," Candice said, and she shared a smile with Jimmy as he finished taking care of Joshua's hand.

After Joshua was all wrapped up, they packed up his gear, got his food down from out of the tree and helped him get his gear on his back, ready to make his way to his ride.

"Please check in with Mountain Rescue when you get to the trailhead. I want to make sure that you're okay. I'm going to be calling in your last coordinates," Candice warned.

Joshua nodded. "Thanks, Ranger Lavoie. I will."

Candice and Jimmy watched as Joshua continued his way down the trailhead.

"Well, if that's the worst of it, I'll be happy," Jimmy said.

"For sure." She shook her head. "Come on, let's make sure the campsite is cleaned and we'll continue on to Snowbowl. It's still another two or three hours before we can stop for the night."

Jimmy nodded.

They packed up the rest of their gear, Candice made the call about Joshua and they made sure they left no trace before continuing on their ascension of the Skyline Trail.

Jimmy walked behind Candice, trying to show her that it wasn't hard for him. That he could handle mountain rescue, but it had been far too long since he'd done this hike with Logan. And even then, he didn't remember it being so brutal.

But then he'd been younger. Not over thirty and unused to the altitude in the mountains. His hip was hurting a bit, but he could manage. He was glad when they took their breaks, or when they met someone else along the trail and checked in with the other hikers—so far, everyone they'd run into had a permit—and there was a couple of times they had to stop because Candice spotted a bear and pulled out her binoculars. That's when they had to give wide berth and make sure the bear knew that they were coming.

One thing Jimmy had forgotten was the spectacular vista as they made their way up from the trailhead toward the snow-covered notch.

There were times when he'd stop to catch his breath, and also just to marvel at the wonder of the place where he'd grown up. High peaks and slender trees, blue glacier-fed lakes. Granite and earth, blue and gold. It really was beautiful.

It made him forget about all the horrors he'd seen while serving. It made everything else seem so small in comparison.

They had spent some time in the Little Shovel campsite to check on hikers before they could continue on to the Snowbowl, so the hike took longer than Candice's estimated two to three hours.

Once they got to Snowbowl, one of the busiest campgrounds on the trail, they went around to check on everyone who was camping before setting up their own campsite. It was then that it hit Jimmy—he and Candice would be sharing a tent.

There wasn't room enough for two tents on their site, as they had to minimize the impact on the environment.

He could tell by the way that Candice was worrying her lip that she hadn't thought of this arrangement, either.

"Do you want me to sleep outside?" He had done that with Logan.

"No. We can make this work. We're adults."

"Right." But he knew that she wasn't completely convinced.

They pitched their tent on the tent pad, grabbed what they needed for their dinner and Jimmy made the small campfire out of the dried brush that was on the ground and homemade fire starters he'd packed, while Candice made her rounds to the six other campsites that were occupied.

It actually shocked Jimmy how busy it was, but then, he probably shouldn't have been surprised.

Summer was a popular time and it was a nice night. There were barely any mosquitos hanging around near the tree line and there wasn't much wind, but it was a bit cold and he was thankful for his warm clothes and his sleeping bag.

Candice came back when he had the fire started.

"Everything good?"

She nodded and pulled out her little folding camp chair, setting it up so she could sit in front of the fire. "Everyone is healthy and they know you're a paramedic should there be any issues in the night."

"Good." He pulled out a couple of bags of freeze-dried meals and added water to them before heating them over the fire. It was food that was easy to pack in and out. It tasted horrible, but it was only for a couple of days.

The sun was beginning to set and it was a clear enough night that he was hoping to see a few stars, though he didn't plan on staying up too late because he was exhausted from their hike.

"Tomorrow night at the lodge will be nice," Candice said. "It's my favorite part of doing the Skyline hike."

"Why's that?" he asked.

"It's a bed to sleep in, indoor plumbing and they feed us. No freeze-dried food for the night."

He grinned. "I can go for that. Your freeze-dried chicken is ready, by the way."

"Yum," she said, making a face, and he laughed.

"At least you don't have to do this hike in the winter."

"No, this trail is shut then, thank goodness, but there have been times when people still barged their way through and we've had to do winter rescues. Not too often, but still. You have to wonder about some people."

"For sure." Jimmy sat down on the ground in front of the fire and tried to pretend that his freeze-dried meal was something better than it was. "What's been your hardest rescue since you started here?"

"Hardest?"

Jimmy nodded. "Tell me about it, so I can learn. I mean, I'm still the newbie here."

She chuckled softly. "Avalanches are always hard. And mudslides. Mudslides are hard."

"Have you ever been in an avalanche?" he asked.

"Once. I was doing a rescue for someone who had been skiing at a high peak—one of those helicopter drops—and before we could extract him, an avalanche struck. I was tethered to my team and we just swam to the side—that's the best you can do." She frowned. "We lost the victim, though. There was nothing we could do and that was my toughest moment. It took so long to let that go." She sighed. "I blamed myself for the longest time."

"You blamed yourself?"

"Of course," she said. "It took a long time for me to realize that some things are out of my control and now I just keep trying to improve, so that I don't lose the next one."

Jimmy pondered that admission for a few minutes.

"What was yours?" she asked.

"What?" he asked.

"You served in the armed forces, you were a paramedic, so what was your hardest moment?"

"My hardest loss was…" It was even hard to say the word. "Logan."

She looked at him then, across the firelight. "Tell me."

And even though he hated talking about it, he just couldn't hold back anymore. There was something about being here with Candice, in a place that had also meant so much to him and her brother, that finally unlocked something inside him. He'd been carrying around that burden for so long. He wanted to be free.

"Our unit was attending a patrol that was down. Logan was the commanding officer and we were working together to get his men out. But then there was an air strike and the helicopter coming to take out wounded men was shot down. Logan and I were blown back by the explosion. When I came to, he was trapped under a wall next to me. The lower half of his body was being crushed and I tried everything—everything I could to save him—but…"

Candice didn't say anything for a few moments. The only sound was his pulse thundering in his ears and a few snaps from their fire as he relived that moment.

"There was nothing you could do," Candice finally said softly.

"No. Nothing. He just slipped away from me." Jimmy tried to hold back the tears.

"I know, Jimmy. We never blamed you. I hope you know that."

He nodded. "Thanks. It was hard to let him go."

"But you were there with him in his final moments and that matters," she said gently. "He had you beside him and I know that would have helped. It would have made him feel like things were going to be okay. There was no one he knew he could count on more than you. You were his best friend."

He glanced up at the sky, trying not to lose control of his emotions in front of her. The stars he'd been looking forward to seeing had started to come out.

"I never get tired of seeing that," Candice whispered, following his upward gaze with her own.

Jimmy glanced at her. She was so kind, so understanding, and it meant a lot to him that she didn't blame him for Logan's death.

He loved her so much. Even after all this time.

"I think I'm going to head to bed." Jimmy picked up the remnants of their meal and the utensils, desperate to busy himself before he did something he would regret. "I'll get our packs up on the pole as soon as I'm done cleaning up."

"Sounds good. I'm beat." Candice put out the fire, covering it with dirt.

Jimmy silently watched the trail of smoke disappear into the darkening sky.

As soon as her head hit her tiny camping pillow, Candice fell asleep. She didn't hear Jimmy come into the tent and get into his own sleeping bag, but she did wake up when she heard him murmuring.

She sat up and glanced at her watch.

It was one in the morning.

It took her a moment for her eyes to adjust

to the darkness and she could see that Jimmy was thrashing and sweating in his sleep.

Not that she blamed him.

She had seen the pain in his face as he talked about Logan's death. It had been hard for her to keep her composure. She knew what had killed Logan—his cause of death had been explained to them at the time—but she didn't know that Jimmy had been right there when it happened.

She also didn't know about the helicopter, which at least explained his aversion to them and why he'd acted so weird.

Candice couldn't even begin to imagine the pain he was going through, or had gone through. It almost broke her to see him grieving her brother still.

She unzipped her bag, scooting out into the coldness of the tent.

"Jimmy," she whispered.

He continued to thrash, locked in his nightmare.

"Candy," he called out, still asleep.

"I'm here."

"I'm sorry," he said. "Logan, I'm sorry. I let you down."

"Shh, no, you haven't." She touched his head and gently stroked his face. "You haven't. I'm here. I'm here."

"Candy?" he murmured, now half-awake.

"Yeah. I'm here."

"Good. Stay with me," he whispered.

"Okay." She pulled her sleeping back closer, snuggling up against Jimmy, her head close to his.

"Candy, I'm sorry."

"I know." She brushed the hair back off his face. "I know and it's okay."

"Good." And he drifted back into sleep.

She knew he wouldn't remember this and that was okay. She was here right now with him and she'd been a fool to think that she wouldn't be.

It was risky putting her heart on the line like this, but she couldn't stop herself.

She was still in love with Jimmy Liu and she always would be.

He'd always had her heart.

Always.

CHAPTER THIRTEEN

IT WAS A long hike to Curator campground and Candice made sure she got up and had her stuff packed before Jimmy knew that she had spent the night curled up beside him. She didn't want him to know that she had been privy to one his nightmares.

They had a long hike of forty-six kilometers ahead of them and she was looking forward to getting up closer to the notch and to the lodge, so she could have a decent night's sleep and some good food.

They had a quick breakfast after Jimmy retrieved their gear from the top of the pole used to avoid bears being attracted to the site.

After finishing packing everything up and filling their filtered water bottles from the stream, they made their way onto the trail. They were the last to leave their campground, as the other hikers had already made an early start after checking in with her.

Some were heading in the same direction, toward the Signal Mountain trailhead, and others were going back down toward the Maligne trailhead. They were still ascending, but tomorrow, as soon as they crested the notch, they would start their descent toward Signal Mountain.

They were right on track to finish on time, provided nothing bad happened, which she was really hoping wouldn't.

Candice was exhausted after a sleepless night, but it was worth it and she knew she was going to sleep well when they got to the lodge later on.

Jimmy was keeping up, and both of them were wearing dark sunglasses to protect their eyes from the sun. The UV rays were a wee bit stronger the higher they ascended. Even though that sun was hot, they wore long sleeves to protect themselves from the sun and the wind.

It was windier today, which slowed their hike, and it was just the two of them on the trail. Them, the mountains and the sky—which was the beauty of backcountry camping in Jasper.

They stopped after four hours to have a drink by a stream and eat something, taking off their packs and sitting down by the trickling water.

"I can see the notch. It's getting closer," Jimmy said, taking a deep breath.

"You're breathing hard. Are you okay?" Candice asked.

Jimmy nodded. "I'm getting used to the elevation again, but don't worry, I'm not showing any signs of AMS. My hip is stiff, but I'm good."

She cocked an eyebrow. "You could be delusional—let me check your hands."

Jimmy smiled and held out her hands. She lifted her sunglasses and examined his nail beds for the signs of cyanosis.

"You're good, but you will tell me if you're having issues, got it?"

"I'm okay, Candice. I swear." He took a bite of his granola bar and looked out over the meadow. "Haven't seen a bear yet today."

"They're still fattening themselves up on shoots, dandelions and grass, and I believe it's caribou calving season still, so they'll be wherever the caribou are." She pulled out her binoculars and scanned the area. "There's nothing as far as these binoculars can see. So that's good."

"I've been watching for tracks, but nothing."

Candice sat down and handed Jimmy the binoculars so he could take a look.

"How long do you think until we get to the

lodge?" he asked casually as he looked around with the binoculars.

"A couple of hours. I don't see any hikers on the horizon at all." She finished her granola bar and packed her garbage away.

"So you mean we might actually get to relax at the lodge tonight?" he teased.

"We got to relax last night. No one was hurt and everyone had a permit. It was all good."

"I forgot to ask yesterday if Joshua made it safe off the trail?"

Candice nodded. "When you were using the facilities, Stu called and told me Joshua got to the hospital."

Jimmy snorted. "Facilities. Sure."

She laughed. "Yeah, they're not the best and not really private. It's rustic."

"Rustic? I think the word you're looking for is primitive."

"What do you expect? This is a national park and this is backcountry camping. If you want facilities you have to get yourself a camper or a recreational vehicle and camp down outside of town or rent a cabin."

"Don't think I haven't thought about it. I'm getting a bit old to be sleeping on the ground."

She rolled her eyes. "Hardly. Shall we go?"

"Yes! Let's get to the lodge." Jimmy handed

her the binoculars and she slung them around her neck.

They clipped their rucksacks back on and headed up the trail. The lodge and the Curator campground were a bit off the Skyline Trail, but both were popular places to spend the night.

When they arrived, they made their rounds in the Curator campground to make sure that everyone there was allowed to be there, and then Jimmy tended to a minor wound on someone's calf that was a bit infected.

After that they hiked to the lodge, where the last little cabin was waiting for them.

Candice's heart sank when she saw it and its one double bed. Her pulse began to race at the thought of having to share a bed with Jimmy tonight.

It's no different than sleeping next to him in the tent.

That was how she had to rationalize it in her mind.

It was for one night.

"Tight quarters," Jimmy remarked.

"Yeah." She worried her bottom lip.

"It'll be okay. I'm just glad it's a real bed and we don't have to even use our sleeping bag. I saw the propane tank, which means heat, right?"

Candice laughed, his enthusiasm breaking the tension that only she, apparently, was feeling. She was relieved about that.

"Yeah, it means heat," she said, dropping her pack into the corner. "Let's wash up and get some dinner."

"Sweet!"

She laughed again and poured the water out of the pitcher into the washstand. She cleaned herself up, trying to keep her back to Jimmy for some privacy, but she couldn't help but peak over her shoulder to watch him change his shirt.

Focus.

She brushed out her hair, braiding it into two braids because it was the easiest to deal with. Once they were both presentable, they made their way out of their private lodge to the main lodge to have dinner.

They passed the stables where the pack animals were kept, then made their way up into the larger lodge, where they joined a group of fifteen other hikers for a home-cooked dinner.

This was Candice's favorite part of the Skyline Trail and it had been some time since she'd been able to come up here and experience this.

Jimmy charmed his way into conversations with the other hikers, a few of whom they had met the previous night at the Snowbowl campground.

The dinner was simple and filling, and soon they made their way back to their lodge. The sun was setting behind the mountain range and they both sat out on their little private deck to enjoy the quiet.

"I could stay here for a few days," Jimmy said with a sigh. "This is a nice way to end a day of hiking."

"It is. It's a nice perk." She glanced over at him and couldn't help but smile. It was nice to sit here with him. She hadn't realized how lonely she'd felt all these years—it was only since Jimmy's return that she'd seen how empty her life had been. Even when she was with Chad, she had been lonely.

She'd been keeping her distance ever since that kiss at Marcus's birthday party, but she missed Jimmy and Marcus. Life was empty and quiet without them.

Logan had been her best friend, but so had Jimmy. And she had missed her best friend.

"What?" Jimmy asked.

"What do you mean?"

"You're smiling at me."

"Is that wrong?" she asked.

"No, I guess just a bit odd since we didn't seem to part on good terms at Marcus's party."

She sighed. "Yeah, I know. I was dealing with a lot of emotions."

"I get that," he said quietly. "I've missed you the last few days."

"Same." Her cheeks heated even more. She got up. "I'm going to go change."

She rushed inside the cabin, embarrassed but also thrilled to hear that he had missed her, too. That he'd been thinking about her.

The door opened and closed behind her.

"Candice, I've never stopping caring for you. I came back to see you once, but you were married and looked so happy. I didn't want to disrupt your life, so I left."

Her heart skipped a beat and she spun around. "You came back?"

"You looked so happy with your husband. I didn't want to intrude." Jimmy reached into his pack and he pulled out a photo. It was worn and crinkled, like it had been viewed a thousand times. "I carried this with me. Logan told me I'd hold you back so I left, but I've never stopped thinking about you."

She couldn't believe it.

He gripped his hand over hers so they were both holding the photo. "Your photo saved me, Candice. So many times."

She handed it back to him so he could pack it away.

"If it hadn't been for Logan…you would've stayed in Jasper?" she asked, emotions swirling through her.

"Yes."

Jimmy couldn't believe that he was admitting this, but he couldn't help himself. Not when it came to Candice. She got under his skin and he was terrified by what it meant, but he wanted to be with her.

Even if it was just for one night, for one moment.

He never wanted to hurt her, but he needed her. Now.

"I can't believe it," she whispered.

"What?" he asked.

"I can't believe that you carried that around."

"Of course I did. I wanted you, too, Candice."

"And now?" she asked.

"I care for you—I always will—but I still don't want to hold you back."

"You're not," she said.

He touched her cheek and ran his hand down her neck. Her pulse was racing a mile a minute—he could feel it under his fingers. She moved closer to him, her fingers lightly brushing over his face, which made him feel like he was on fire.

He closed his eyes, trying to regain control over his senses, knowing it was Candice touching him. Something that he'd dreamed about for so long.

"Jimmy," she whispered, her voice catching in her throat.

He cupped her face and pulled her close, tight against his body.

He wanted to kiss her again, like they had before. Only he didn't want this kiss to end. This is what passion with Candice tasted like. He remembered it so keenly. It was sweet and honeyed and he wanted it all.

It rocked him to his core. He didn't want this moment to end. He wanted more.

Oh, God.

"Candice, I don't know if we should," he said, even though he wanted to.

"Do you not want me now?" she asked breathlessly.

"I do."

Candice touched his chest. "I think we should, because I want you, Jimmy. I always have."

"I want you, too. I can't help it. I've always wanted you."

And it was true.

He wanted Candice.

She was here. He was here.

And he wanted her.

Candice melted in his arms again.

This was what she wanted—to be swept up in his arms.

She wasn't one-hundred-percent sure he wouldn't hurt her, but tonight she was willing to take the risk. Just like she had the night they first made love ten years ago.

She was ready and wanted to be with Jimmy in this moment. Again.

Righting a wrong.

She'd always wanted Jimmy and had never felt for another man what she felt for him. It was fierce, overpowering. It scared her and thrilled her how she burned for him after all this time. He woke her up when she hadn't even realized she'd been asleep.

"Candice, if you're sure."

"I am."

She shrugged out of her shirt. "Touch me," she whispered.

"Oh, God. Candice." Jimmy scooped her up and carried her the short distance to the bed, lying her down, pressing his kisses over her body. Over her lips, her neck and lower.

"You make me feel alive again," he whispered and then kissed her deeply, their tongues entwining.

They made quick work getting out of their clothes so they could be skin-to-skin. She ran her hands over his body, touching him, reveling in the sensation of being with him again. Even if it made her vulnerable. She ran her hands over his scars, and it made her breath catch in her throat to see what damage had been done to him.

He caught her hand. "I'm okay now. I'm here."

She nodded. "I know."

She opened her legs for him to settle between her thighs. She was already wet with need and she arched her hips toward him, wanting him to touch her.

To take her.

Wanting to feel all of him.

"I don't have protection," he groaned.

"I'm on birth control."

"You're sure?"

"Yes." She bucked her hips, making him moan. "I'm sure."

Jimmy kissed her again, deeply, his hands on her body branding her skin where he touched her. His touch making her blood sing.

"You're so beautiful," he murmured against

her neck. His hand slid between her legs, strok-
ing her and driving her wild with need.

"I want you inside me."

"Oh, God, I want that, too."

He covered her body with his and thrust.

Candice cried out. She couldn't stop herself.
Being with him was overwhelming. It's what
she had always wanted.

"You're so tight," he moaned.

She moved her hips, urging him as he moved
slowly at first, when all she wanted was it hard
and fast.

She wanted Jimmy to possess her, to take
her.

Only him.

He moved faster, making her cling to him
as he took her with urgent need. The sweet release built deep inside her and she succumbed.
Pleasure overtook her as he continued thrust-
ing until he stilled, his release coming shortly
after hers.

He rolled to the side and she curled up next
to him, listening to him breathe in the darkness. It was comfortable. Safe.

And that safety scared her.

The last time she'd felt this way all the people she cared about were still alive.

"Candice?" he asked. "Are you crying?"

"No."

She sat up and brushed away the tears. "I'm fine."

Only that was a lie. She knew she couldn't trust him with her heart...but she'd lost it to him, anyway.

CHAPTER FOURTEEN

LOUD BANGING BROUGHT her out of her slumber.

She didn't know when she'd fallen asleep, just that she'd fallen asleep curled up against Jimmy and they didn't have their clothes on.

"Ranger Lavoie!" The frenzied shout came from outside.

Candice jumped out of bed and threw on her glasses. It was five in the morning, and the light was just tinging the sky.

The banging continued.

"What's going on?" Jimmy asked groggily.

"Ranger Lavoie!" the urgent voice yelled.

"Coming!" Candice shouted. She frantically began pulling on her clothes so that she could answer the door.

She opened the door. "What's wrong."

"A hiker fell in the lake—we don't know how long they've been there, so we're doing CPR."

"Okay. We're coming." Candice scrambled and grabbed her satellite phone.

"What's going on?" Jimmy asked as he pulled on his gear.

"Hiker fell in the lake. I'm calling the helicopter."

A strange look passed on Jimmy's face. "What?"

"They're doing CPR down by the lake. See what you can do," she said.

"On my way." Jimmy grabbed his pack and headed out the door to follow the manager of the lodge to the lake.

"Mountain Rescue," Stu's voice said over the phone.

"Stu, it's Lavoie. I need a helicopter stat to Shovel Pass."

"I'll dispatch one right away."

Candice was glad the lodge was well known so she didn't have to give her coordinates and that the helicopter would have lots of room to land.

She pulled on her boots and grabbed her pack, heading to the lake. It was foggy out and she could see how a hiker making one wrong move might stumble off the path into the lake. She moved along the path she knew so well and came across Jimmy, who had taken over CPR for the hiker.

"What can I do?" Candice asked, kneeling down on the opposite side of the hiker.

"I brought a defibrillator. I need that."

Candice nodded and went into Jimmy's pack, finding the defibrillator at the top. He was still doing compressions and breathing in the women's mouth.

She could hear the helicopter. It wasn't far out.

"Take over compressions for me," Jimmy said as he began to attach the defibrillator.

Candice took over.

"Okay. Clear, Candice."

Candice moved and Jimmy used the defibrillator.

There was a flutter of the woman's eyes.

"It's working," Jimmy said. "Continue with compressions."

Candice continued and then there was a cough and gurgling as the woman tried to bring up lake water. They rolled her into the recovery position.

"Good, good," Jimmy whispered. "You're going to be okay."

Candice pulled out a blanket from the bag and they wrapped the woman up to prevent hypothermia.

The woman's husband was close by. "Is she going to be okay?"

"We're going to take her to the hospital in

the helicopter," Candice said. "You can come with us."

The man nodded.

Jimmy was frowning.

She knew that it had to do with his fear of helicopters, but now was not the time to placate him. The had a job to do.

The helicopter landed, and the blades kept running.

Stu got out with a backboard and they worked to get the hiker ready to be taken down the mountain. They loaded her and her husband in the medical helicopter and Candice tossed in their gear to Stu. When she looked back, she saw Jimmy standing at a distance.

Frozen.

He still had his gear.

"We've got to go, Jimmy," Candice said.

"I can't."

"You have to. I know you're afraid, but you can do this."

His eyes narrowed. "What do you know of my fear? You don't know anything. You weren't there. You don't know how it feels."

"You're right. I don't, but Jimmy, we have to go *now*," she said firmly.

Jimmy pursed his lips and nodded. He climbed on board, but she could tell that he was on edge. That this was too much for him as he took the noise-canceling headphones and buckled himself in.

"All good, Nigel!" Candice shouted.

Nigel gave the thumbs-up and the helicopter rose off the mountain and made its way down the rest of the trail, heading toward Jasper rather than Signal Mountain.

Candice was a little disappointed they wouldn't get to finish the trail, but this was what they were here for. She'd let the rangers know when they landed that they were unable to finish the rest of the trail from Curator Lake down to the Signal trailhead, and the rangers would take care of the rest.

Jimmy wasn't looking at her and she knew that he was having a hard time with this. She tried to get him to look at her, but he couldn't.

Or he wouldn't.

Her heart sank. This reminded her of what had happened that night ten years ago, when he'd left. He became distant, cool, and wouldn't look at her. She'd had no idea what he was feeling.

She was angry that she was being made to feel so uncertain, that she was losing control of her rational thought and letting her anxiety take over because of him…again.

She hated this. She swore she'd never let

anyone make her feel this way again. And yet here she was.

This was a mistake.

The helicopter landed on the helipad, where doctors were waiting to take the patient and her husband straight into the hospital. The patient was breathing on her own, but they had to make sure her lungs were clear and that she overcame her hypothermia.

Jimmy told the doctors what he had done and passed off the case.

Candice climbed out of the helicopter with their gear. They could head back to their homes from here, and Nigel and Stu could head back to the airfield. They walked silently off the helipad toward the parking lot as Nigel flew the helicopter up and away.

Once it was in the distance Jimmy turned toward her. It was clear he was angry.

"I didn't appreciate that."

"What?" she snapped.

"Ordering me on the helicopter, especially after I told you what happened."

"You're a paramedic. You had to come."

"So is Stu and he was there."

"You worked on the patient!" Candice snarled. "See sense, Liu. You had to get on that helicopter. There wasn't time to be afraid.

And you knew beforehand that helicopters were part of this job!"

He glared at her as they walked away from the hospital. "It's nothing to do with fear. I have post-traumatic stress disorder, Candice. I couldn't get on that helicopter."

"Is your PTSD going to continue to affect your job like this?" she asked, knowing how harsh she was being even as she said it.

"So now here comes the boss hat." He shook his head.

"Jimmy, it's important. If it is going to be an obstacle, you need help."

"I've had help. I know how to deal with my PTSD and I disclosed this information when I was hired for the job. I got on the helicopter, didn't I?"

"You did get on, but not without a fight. I'm worried about you, Jimmy."

"You don't need to worry about me," he said quickly. "Not anymore. I won't hold you back, Candice. It's clear you can live your life just fine without me."

She was taken aback. Her heart skipped a beat and her stomach sank like a rock. This was exactly how it had happened last time.

He was letting her go. Again.

"You're not holding me back," she said.

"No. You're right. I'm not," he snapped. "You're holding yourself back!"

"What's that supposed to mean?"

"Why did you stay here, Candice? There's nothing for you here. Go, make your dreams come true. Don't be so afraid to leave."

It was like a slap to the face.

"You're here, Jimmy," she said. "What if I want to stay?"

He shook his head. "Don't stay for me."

"Well, I'm not the only one hiding from the world." Her voice trembled. "Have you even dealt with Logan's death? Have you even gone to see him since you got here? You say you're not free, but you are. You have a family, a child. You can go anywhere with him."

"Yes, I have a child. I had another one, but you didn't bother telling me about that, did you? You were afraid to tell me about our baby, but I had the right to know."

A tear slid down her cheek. "Yeah, you did have that right, but I had the right to know why you left me. Logan may have thought he did the right thing telling you to leave, but he didn't. It was my life. My choices."

"Then go live it, Candice. Go."

She didn't know what to say to that.

"I'll see you at work." She turned on her heel and walked away from him, trying not to cry.

Candice was angry she'd given her heart to him again and been burned once more.

Jimmy watched her walk away as it began to rain. He was getting soaked, but he didn't care. He hated himself for what he'd done.

For breaking his promise to Logan by falling in love with Candice.

For ruining things with her a second time.

Jimmy didn't go after her. Instead he headed home. He needed to have a hot shower and he needed to get into a change of clothing.

When he walked into his house, his mother was shocked to see him.

"You're soaked through!" she exclaimed.

"Yeah," he said, exhausted. "Where's Marcus?"

"Napping. You weren't supposed to be home yet."

"We had to airlift someone off the mountain."

His mother pursed her lips. "Did you get on the helicopter?"

"I did."

"That's progress."

"Is it? I almost didn't, Mom." He scrubbed a hand over his face.

"But you did," his mother said. "Go have a hot shower and dry off. You're dirty and soaked and things will seem clearer once you're clean and dry."

"Will they?"

Liena smiled. "They will."

Jimmy wasn't so sure of that. He headed upstairs and went to have a shower. It felt good to rinse off the mountain.

As he stood there with the water rolling down his skin, all he could think about was Candice and what she had said.

That she was still here.

What was he so afraid of?

He wasn't a burden.

In the end, he'd been the one Logan had asked to take care of his sister.

Promise me one thing. Take care of Candy for me.

Logan's voice was so clear in his head.

He got out of the shower and dried himself off. He had to find Candice. He had to make things right. She was the one for him. She always had been. He'd go anywhere, do anything, to make a family with her. He couldn't walk away from her again.

Logan had been his best buddy, but Candice had also always been there for him.

She was his best friend.

And he couldn't live without her.

As he dressed, his phone started vibrating with a call from Mountain Rescue.

"Candice?" he asked, answering the phone.

"No, it's Stu, there's been a mudslide and the helicopter Candice was piloting went down."

"What?"

"I'm coming by with the rig. It's all hands on deck."

"I'm ready."

Jimmy's stomach sank to the soles of his feet, his heart hammering. And as he glanced at his phone he saw the messages that had come through while he was in the shower.

He cursed.

And he prayed she was okay.

I can't lose her.

He'd lost her once before, he wouldn't lose her again.

He was ready and out the door as the rig pulled up, his gear in his hands.

"What happened?" he asked quickly. "The details in the message weren't clear."

Stu looked worried. "There was a mudslide on the highway. Candice went to check it out and after she took off to head back to base we got word of the mayday and lost contact."

"What about the mudslide?"

"Thankfully no one was involved as there

was no one driving along that section of the highway."

Jimmy worried his lip. "Was she alone?"

"No, Nigel was with her, but not flying. Kate was on board, too."

Stu raced along the highway out of town and down the Icefields Parkway. It took them a good twenty minutes to get to a point where Jimmy could see a plume of smoke rising from the ground.

His stomach knotted and his pulse raced.

Oh, God.

As they rounded the corner, he could see a wall of mud and where the RCMP had barricaded off the road. They moved to let them through.

The helicopter was a mess and on fire, smoking. He could make out Kate and Nigel sitting off to the side of the road, but he couldn't see Candice.

"No," Jimmy whispered.

His stomach sank and he felt like he couldn't breathe. Like the wall of mud was suffocating him.

No, he couldn't lose her.

Stu pulled over and Jimmy bolted from the ambulance, panic driving him as he made his way through the mess of debris and smoke.

Nigel was bleeding from a head wound and

Kate was lying on a tarp with other paramedics dealing with her.

"She's over there," Nigel said, seeing his frantic face.

Jimmy nodded and made his way through the crowd. Finally, he saw Candice, soaking wet with a makeshift sling, talking to an RCMP officer.

"Candice!" he shouted above the sound of the drizzle.

She spun around, her face scratched up. "Jimmy?"

Jimmy stopped in front of her, resisting the urge to pull her into his arms. "Are you okay?"

"I could be worse. You should be looking after Nigel. Where is your gear?"

"Stu has Nigel and Kate. I was worried about you."

She smiled, but her face was guarded. "I'm fine."

"You could've died."

"But I didn't. I landed the helicopter when I saw there was engine trouble. It was a rough landing and as we were getting out the helicopter it caught on fire and we got caught up in another small mudslide. We have to get to the hospital. Nigel has an open wound."

Jimmy sighed. "Thank God you're okay."

"I think I sprained my wrist, but, yeah, I'm

okay." She smiled. "You weren't answering your page."

"I was in the shower." He looked up at the sky. "Fat lot of good that did me."

She laughed gently. "Don't let this accident interfere with your job. Look, I know I was hard on you, but you're a good paramedic. I don't want to lose you."

"I don't care about the damn helicopter," Jimmy said. He took a step toward her. "It was you I was worried about."

"Me? Why?" Her eyes were wide and he could see that she was trembling.

"Because I love you, Candice Lavoie. I always have. And when I heard your helicopter went down, I thought I'd lost you. I can't live without you. I was a fool. I'll go anywhere, do anything to be with you. I'm sorry, but I won't leave you again. I need you."

Candice took a step back, her breath catching in her throat. She couldn't quite believe what she was hearing. Tears stung her eyes.

"You—you what?"

"I love you, Candice. I always have. Logan was my friend, but you are my best friend. You always have been and I was too blind to see it. I walked away from you once before, but I can't walk away this time. I can't. I need you in my life. You're my family and I want you to be a part of Marcus's family, too. I can't lose you."

Tears started streaming down her face. "You love me?"

"I do. I've never stopped loving you. I was a fool to take so long to realize it."

A lump formed in her throat and she began to cry. "I… I've been so alone and… I've always loved you too, Jimmy. I've never stopped loving you. I was just… I was so afraid of getting hurt and losing the only family I have left in this world. I was afraid of losing you."

Jimmy cupped her face in his hands and wiped away her tears in the rain. "You'll never lose me. You'll always have me, that is, if you still want me?"

Candice smiled, her heart skipping a beat. "I do. I want you, Jimmy. I always have and I always will."

Jimmy bent down and kissed her, and though she never liked to let her guard down when she was working, she couldn't help but melt in his arms and kiss him back.

This was where she belonged. With him.

She was finally home.

EPILOGUE

One year later

CANDICE PARKED THE car in her driveway and saw that Jimmy and Marcus were sitting on the front steps, waiting for her to come home, like they often did. Especially when she and Jimmy weren't working together.

Not that they had been working together since they'd gotten married.

Candice had stepped back from her job as head of Mountain Rescue to take online courses and finish her degree. And they had plans to spend the winter in Edmonton so that she could finish her premed course and enrol in medical school.

Of course, now that might have to be postponed, but Candice was quite okay with that.

"Hi, Candy," Marcus shouted from the porch.

"Hey, how was your day?" Candice asked as Marcus ran over and gave her a big hug.

"Good. Năinai and I went to the park and did crafts!" Marcus showed her the painting he made. "It's us!"

"Although there's an extra person in our family," Jimmy teased.

Marcus glared at him. "Năinai said the number was just right."

"It's a great picture." Candice kissed the top of Marcus's head and took the picture from him while he went back to playing.

Jimmy chuckled and came down the steps to give her a kiss. "You're going to give our son a complex. And clearly my mother is having some issues with counting."

"Maybe not," Candice teased.

Jimmy cocked an eyebrow. "What's going on?"

"I had my check up with Dr. Zwart today. Regular physical stuff."

"Right…" Jimmy said, taking a step back.

"Your mother is quite perceptive. She obviously knew before I did."

Jimmy looked at the painting and then looked at her. "Are you serious?"

Candice smiled. "Yes. So I'll have to delay medical school for the time being. Stu said he'd have me back in a heartbeat to do the paperwork at Mountain Rescue since he hates it so much."

"We're going to have a baby?" Jimmy asked, still stunned.

"Yep. Should come early next year."

"A winter baby in Jasper," Jimmy groaned and then he grinned. "A baby!"

"I know, but I do have the best paramedic in Jasper as my husband," she said, putting her arms around his neck.

Jimmy grinned. "That you do."

"So are you happy?" she asked.

"I am." He kissed her gently and then touched her belly. "Very happy."

"Me, too."

"So why don't we go tell Marcus that his *nǎinai* was right and there is an extra person coming?"

Candice chuckled. "I'd like that, but you know he's not going to be surprised. He'll just call you out on it. He's exactly like you."

Jimmy sighed. "I know, and I hope our next kid is just like you."

"You know he or she will probably do the same."

Jimmy laughed. "I hope so. I certainly hope so."

They walked hand in hand up the porch to share the news with Marcus and let him know that he was going to be a big brother.

Candice was happy. She was no longer alone. She had her family.

And, together, they were home.

* * * * *

If you enjoyed this story, check out these other great reads from Amy Ruttan

Reunited with Her Hot-Shot Surgeon
Baby Bombshell for the Doctor Prince
Pregnant with the Paramedic's Baby
Royal Doc's Secret Heir

All available now!